Soaking Red

Jacob Russell Dring

Author's Note

Originally written and self-published as a 6x9 paperback on October 14th, 2010, *Soaking Red* quickly became my most-read and most-reviewed book, remaining so to this day. I've included reviews for the original on the next page, as I did in 2012 copies of the book.

Heavily inspired by my newfound obsession with Deftones, namely their Diamond Eyes album, the book acted as a turning point in my style, striving to write more poetically and with an emphasis on visceral, emotive imagery.

As proud of the original as I was for many years to come, eventually my evolution and improvement as a writer made it harder to appreciate in hindsight. It felt amateurish and a struggle to read in places, from both a writing and structural standpoint. However, my adoration of the characters, plot, and the underlying themes have remained passionate as ever.

Hence my return.

This version of *Soaking Red* is not just a revision, but a reinvention. Only now does it feel worthy of the praise that the original received. Fans of the 2010 version, I hope you enjoy this iteration just as much if not more, and can see—can feel—the improvements made.

Thank you so much for reading.

What Some Readers Had to Say About
Soaking Red (2010)

"[Jacob's] words are unfiltered from a mind that we may never truly understand but should never take for granted."
– Michael A., July 2010

"Soaking Red is an honest window to true passion and must be read with an open mind. Once you do, you'll discover the greatness of this story and the satisfaction of embarking on one of the most unique experiences book reading has to offer."
– Mark V., July 2010

"This story is simply electrifying….From the moment I read the first sentence I couldn't put this tale down. From the beginning all the way to the climactic end. Like a true writer, [Jacob] never wastes a word….This book is a must-read. Period! "
– Samantha B., October 2010

"This self-published work achieves something both strange and original rarely found from a publishing house: an amorous indulgence which both creeps then explodes into a nightmare of the macabre."
– John D., September 2011

I

My hand swiped the mirror, slow and meditative. The dust pushed aside, as if it was never there to begin with. Like a windshield wiper, I cleared the path for a better look. Not outside, though. Nor through. But right back at me. The mirror's reflection held me in its eye. An expressionless face of subdued contemplation.

I was neither sad, nor mad.

Content, perhaps.

Not alone. That, I was. The key to it all.

I continued staring at the reflection in the mirror. That face, I'd seen a thousand times prior, but for once it felt as if a stranger. Not only to me, but to this world. An extraterrestrial having landed on Earth and being more affable than bitter, as portrayed in movies.

So, what should I have done?

I welcomed it. I embraced it. I adapted and adjusted until I became the man I was. Someone very loved, admired and even revered. The notion sent chills through me, and tickled a smile upon my face.

That very face.

And yet, I was leagues from perfect.

Lurking there, beneath my strengths and blessings, were weaknesses like sugar in the gas tank. We were all human, it was only a matter of not being defined by our foibles.

Hell, just look at me.

My face was a self-published book cover with a lot of time, and trials of error put into it. Crafted well, mildly attractive, but only hooking certain audiences. Others wouldn't think twice—they would pass right over me. Not even a second glance. No desire to read the inner pages, let alone scrutinize my dust jacket. A brief synopsis of me, my life, my experiences and my emotions.

The shallow end of the pool, not even worth their big toe.

They would just keep on walking.

Judgments were so easily passed when you're not the one being judged.

I wouldn't criticize others, though.

That was Simon Cowell and Roger Ebert's job.

My eyes lingered on my features in a moment of pensive, generous vanity. I admired the beauty that was there, both beneath the surface, seeping through pores perceived and unseen, as well as the exterior. Arms still at my side, I slowly appreciated this beauty. My gaze doing the work, the delicate labor of self-love. I squeezed it like a soft blanket. A one-hundred-percent cotton throw with cashmere edges and Kevlar threads.

Because nobody's inner beauty could be shattered.

I didn't care what other people might say, I'd protest. No amount of tribulations could defeat that which lied beneath.

Now, let's really look at me.

The palm and side of my hand wore the thin film of dust from the mirror. I lifted it above the sink, thumb out, and turned it over. A huff through my nostrils, and a skewed smirk. The frontline of dust at the edge of my hand was only the first wave of troops to the entire battalion of grime I had to bear.

And the dust was transient.

My flaws were there to stay.

But I didn't combat them. They weren't to be hunted with torches and pitchforks.

I lifted my gaze and stared back at myself.

Through opposing shores of dust, an interlude of clarity. The cleared mirror was perfect there, untarnished and genuine.

That which returned its gaze, although I knew it was me, for a moment seemed like a different creature. A beautifully grotesque hybrid of much more valuable humans in the world. But the aberration returning my stare looked far more familiar than any resemblance.

He looked like Lucas Bravo.

Yeah, that was it.

A befitting name since birth, I'd been told.

Now, some twenty-eight years later…

I was actually loved for being him.

My eyes studied the features that made this man who he was.

Lean, but not gaunt. Arguably unhealthy habits didn't make an unhealthy human. I was, of course, more than my frame.

Hazel eyes were dependent on light exposure, favoring brown in the dark and green when the shadows scattered. Dark, thin eyebrows. Very short brown hair. Black plugs in each earlobe, five-eighths. Skinny nose, narrow chin. Barely existent stubble, ear to ear, with a patch of thicker hair below my bottom lip. You'd not even realize I had a narrow chin had I not said it.

Then again, that's what we were as people. Perceptions and realities, always skating a thin line.

It almost made me smile.

And reminded me of the canvas I'd turned myself into, over the years. An artistic expression of how I felt inside. The only way I knew how, given that I had no talent in the arts.

Tattoos mottled my chest, back, arms, and legs. Not every inch covered, though. My flesh was the easel, and everything else was just an allotment of empty spaces for various ideas and emotions.

A vivid blend of colors, with the occasional dominance of solid blackwork.

A gold dragon with a wolf's head, slinking through an emerald jungle, composed my left arm. The full moon peeked through trees at its tail, engulfing my shoulder. A large dark feather, in varying shades of black and gray, alone along my right triceps. Below, a blue-steel anchor on my right forearm, an attached brown rope coiling up my elbow and around my bicep.

I didn't need to turn around to see the words arching across my upper back. The sight, the knowledge, was buried there, in my mind's eye.

Luctor et Emergo.

Latin for "I struggle and emerge."

Punctuating this on either side were immense wings curving down from the backs of my shoulders. They had endured many transformations over the years. When I was twenty-two, they were skeletal with beige coloration. Three and a half years later, I had light gray, angelic feathers attached. At twenty-seven they received a reddish hue, with ember spots at the edges.

The little space that remained on my left arm was gifted symbols of my late parents.

A whitetail buck's head emerging from a tribal arrowhead, its antlers beautifully crafted to show age and distinction. Below, a peony floated in a pond.

Full color, as they deserved.

My legs were not finished.

An oceanic panorama swallowed my left knee, calf, and shin. A hammerhead gliding through the waters, its crescent jaws above my ankle. Always nipping at my heels, so to speak.

Keeping me on my toes.

Not an easy task, nor a job for just one beast.

Opposite, Hermes wings adorned my right ankle. His Caduceus stretched up my shin, a painful experience not yet finished. The snake coiling around the blade had a wide path, extending to my calf, too. All partly colored.

A completely black silhouette of a boy playing the trombone occupied my right abdomen, roughly five inches tall. Work on my ribs that had been less than pleasant, but fitting given that the boy had once been me. The mouth of his trombone expanded into a flock of blackbirds that migrated to my other ribcage.

Below, just beneath my beltline, read *EST 1983*.

And far, far from the most important piece.

Covering my unremarkable chest was a tattoo that had quickly become my most significant. It had taken from me a lot of pain, time, and money.

And love.

In graffiti style, it read *SOAKING RED*, blended with a pair of three-letter initials that linked together.

Mine and my girlfriend's.

Of course, I didn't see all of this in the mirror.

The cleared path between seas of dust on the mirror offered me only a glimpse of my shoulders and up. It was generous for even that amount.

The other sects of soot could be likened to my youth, as it were. To how I used to perceive myself, and life in general. The world around me, and the people who inhabited it.

And even that had been a foolish concept.

Too long.

It took me too long to see that it was the other way around. I inhabited their world, and this place was not even ours to begin with.

We were just passersby.

Grasping this came in waves. I gradually met people who changed my views and how I treated myself.

Leila was easily the most momentous.

In all honesty, as I've been known to be a particularly forward guy, *no*—I didn't believe in soulmates. Neither in the word, nor in marriage. The concept of a true, genuine love, however, didn't evade me. It was a belief, one of my very few faiths, which I would hold onto until the end of time, and any eras that might follow.

Love was something I condemned when I was younger, unfortunately. My own experiences with its fallacies had worn me down and erected guards instead of open arms.

To make matters worse, I had been a victim of self-inflicted rebellious tendencies and recklessness. Given, admittedly, some of these inclinations still existed, but now at least they didn't sink in an ocean of tar. No, now they swam freely, in a sea extracted of inhibitions, waves eddying towards absolute liberation.

And I had Leila to thank for most of this.

If you're an antagonist of clichés and feta—arguably one of the best cheeses—then you might want to turn back now.

But blame Leila—she infected me with it.

And I embraced the virus, happily.

The love I developed for Leila, like a speeding bullet the moment I met her, and what her own affection had since created in me, gave way to an inimitable bliss.

Day to day peace, y'all.

I called her my girlfriend simply for the orthodox. For lack of a better word, although I'd argue for *lover*, if any collection of syllables had to be chosen. I personally despised the term soulmate, because I believed everyone's soul was their own to cultivate. No matter how much in love two people were, their souls weren't real estate to barter with.

As far as I saw it, whenever two people made love, or fucked, it was strictly a physical act. Two vessels colliding. But of course, even this carnal experience wasn't necessarily devoid of emotion and thought, two factors that tended to intensify any such event.

Although, if more body than mind, it would merely be an act of doing the dirty deed.

Which, mind you, I was not against.

How could I be?

But with her…it was less black and white.

It seemed like every time we stripped down and meshed together, we involved not only our flesh but our psyches and emotions in the sheerest of forms.

Dare I even say purest?

No. Neither of us were an inkling of perfect. It could be inferred by a third party that we thrived on our faults, and despite moments of purity in our love, it was ultimately adulterated by vulgarity and sin.

Religion. Not a tome of a topic I ever cared to dive into, with anyone. With Leila, it all sort of unfurled in the act of learning each other's ropes.

Monotheism didn't touch us with a ten-foot pole nor would we reach out to it. We just went with the flow of things, never going heavy on faith.

Unless it was the faith we placed in each other. It kept us afoot, and constantly adapting, our bond evolving to survive this world.

I of course spoke as if we had met centuries ago, operating on some sort of Coppola vision of Dracula's love. When in reality we were merely two years deep, despite the old soul feeling heard in song and read in fairytales.

Leila and I were just…

Humans.

Humans, who felt like more.

Now you know me. Leila Pierce was a whole other story, and an individual I only wished I could compare to. From my perspective, at this point in our lives, I'd like to believe we were two peas in a pod. That we fed off of each other, both literally and figuratively, that our personalities mirrored when they didn't clash, opposing magnets wishing for the destruction of Earth if it meant we could just melt together.

And we would.

And we did.

Still, Leila was Leila.

Like myself, or anyone for that matter, she had nonetheless been compared to others. Models, singers.

She would act flattered, but never more than how she felt beheld by my eye, and my hands of reverence.

More often than not it was I who felt unworthy. That, of course, always passed.

In looking at Leila, though, it seemed momentarily plausible.

Any memory of her sufficed, and that was putting it lightly. I found myself smiling…to myself…as I wandered, aimlessly, into a labyrinth of lovely memories. Her tattooed form, a healthily pallid, lean figure, every inch of her body enticing to each of my senses, and tempting into existence a sixth.

A sudden breeze worked its way into the bathroom, snaking around my bare legs and chilling my…

The cold had infiltrated the cabin somehow.

Thank you, nature. Now go fuck yourself.

There I was, standing naked before a dusty mirror above a pedestal sink, in a dimly lit bathroom. Slash bedroom. It was a single chamber altogether. An unusual floorplan, but something to be admired. The meshing of intimacy over privacy.

Behind me, though, was what made the cabin feel like a home above anything else.

Well, a cabin and a lair.

"Did you just open a window?"

I posed the question without looking away from the unconventionally handsome man in the mirror.

"Maaaaybe," she drawled, ever so adorably, from behind me. Likely on the bed. There was an undeniable, tangible comfort in her tone.

The woman was my walking, talking, breathing room and board.

With a sigh, I couldn't help but smirk.

It showed up in the mirror and for a brief moment I reveled where we were. Not just the small cabin but the glade which it occupied, a little blemish in the thick woodland surrounding it. A slice of heaven, hell, and everything that came—quite literally—between them.

Leila had referred to it as a green quilt of trees, with one patch missing, and the getaway cabin we were renting was that patch. She then called it the eye of a storm, a notion I stole from her mouth with a larcenous kiss. Intent on proving that it was just the opposite, should we so choose.

In a more straightforward manner, she had been right. It was our escape from the real world, a storm which we had no control over. Here, however, we were at the helm.

With summer over our shoulders, autumn was beginning its descent into winter. Early October was upon us, but most of the trees were still green. The frigidity of death had yet seized the region. Nor would it conquer us; even in our most idle stages, we wouldn't submit to complete inertia.

We had a complicated relationship with the cold.

Despite our lust for warmer climates, there was something evocative about lower temperatures. How it stirred in me the *we*, the *us*, the basal urge to fit together, to bind our bodies while the shadows of the forest basked in curiosity.

Leila cracking the window in our bedroom was an obvious enough gesture.

Had she wished for a docile passion, she wouldn't have welcomed nature's cold breath into our autumn home.

The cold called for relentless, unrestrained, fervent sex. Some people wouldn't even call it coitus. It was something more feral, an act deserved of a dominion of beasts.

It certainly wasn't lovemaking.

Which had its place in our lives, for sure.

But when the cold knocked at our door, and it came in so many different fashions, we were blind to the values of making love. It paled in comparison to the lechery bubbling inside of us.

In that moment, we saw lovemaking as no different than the shallow end. It was the slow lane. Lovemaking was decaf. Using a condom. Waiting a half-hour to go swimming after you ate. Setting alarms on your day off from work.

Lovemaking could also be bliss, and rapture in the flesh.

Not when the cold nibbled at our skin, though.

And Leila had opened that window for a good fucking reason.

Bad things, with good intentions.

Very bad things.

Like pleasing the unpleasant.

Fuck, we were made for each other.

"You coming or what?" Her voice beckoned me. A mellifluous tone with a lick of attitude.

I smirked and turned on my heel, facing the bed. Taking it all in. The sight of her sprawled on her side atop the sheets, our white wool comforter pushed over. Her body and beauty—a gift from the deity of lust.

"We haven't even gotten there yet," I said, standing naked before her, cold yet warm all at once.

She simpered and I wouldn't let my own archaic smile falter. I did however glimpse the window behind her, on the wall beside the bed. She hadn't cracked it, exactly. She had opened the whole damn thing. Now, more than just late morning daylight gushed into the cabin. The cold air from outside intruded our home away from home, filling the room with its crispness.

And we bathed in it without aversion.

My eyes returned to Leila, and there they wanted to stay indefinitely.

A compassionate, creative, vigorous woman who was zealous about everything she loved, and yet could hate-fuck the soul right out of me. It was all for the sake of the moment, though. Leila was never without heart, and though two years younger than me, she was in so many ways more…established.

Almost as if she had it all figured out.

She didn't, and would confess as much. But me? I was no more a mystery to her than the Sunday cross-words.

Every time I looked at her, however, I was genuinely blown away. I found myself lost in her smallest details, weaving through mazes of subterranean beauty. Be it under the raw moonlight, creeping above stark canopies, or the subtle glow of a bedside lamp with a faulty cord. She was never anything shy of poetry.

Every time we kissed, I would swear I knew the flavor of ambrosia, that the food of the Gods existed here on Earth and I had it at my fingertips. Or the precipice of my tongue, for that matter. Every time we tasted each other, I tried to forget I was still alive, because that level of transcendence was only meant for the dead.

Was I exaggerating a little?

Sure. A little. But that was as far as I'd go.

"You just had to open the whole window, didn't you?" I said, my voice low and smooth. It billowed out in front of me, visible in the growing cold.

Leila just smiled, dimples in either cheek. Thulian lips pressed together, veiling her white teeth. Every inch of her delectable.

A sort of humanoid white tiger lying there on the bed, striped in tattoos and a predatory nature teeming in her brown eyes. A pigmentation understated since the beginning of time, and underestimated. The power in Leila's eyes held me fast as stone, but she was far too gorgeous to behold a Medusa comparison. Her jet black hair and dark features stunningly contrasted a pale complexion, which in the winter was not unlike snow.

Only softer, if one could imagine.

I could write whole volumes' worth of dramatizations when it came to Leila. With scrolls instead of pages, unfurling to a length comparable to her hair—

Before June.

She had cut it real short then, after it had grown down to tickle the dimples of Venus on her lower back. To better situate her livelihood in the heat of summer, she wielded scissors like Edward and gave it the chop.

She said we would both have to "adjust" to it being so short at the time. I didn't know what she was on about, I adored any changes she brought upon herself. They never diminished her beauty, internally or otherwise, so I was sold.

"What if I were to shave my head?" She had asked, her mouth struggling not to grin at the idea.

"Then we'll truly be two peas in a pod," I had replied, jokingly but genuinely all the same.

Cue laughter.

Cue arms. And lips. And tongues.

I just kept looking at her. Time passed here in the cabin like no other. We were in our own world, no duties knocking at our door, no urgency nipping at our heels.

Good—because I wanted to savor every inch of her in every glimpse I could snatch.

Her hair currently floated millimeters above her bare shoulders.

Leaving sufficient room for her Angel and Devil to sit. I liked to imagine they were old friends, who enjoyed sitting by the fire and sharing cups of acid tea while telling stories from their respective realms. While mine probably fucked each other silly whenever they got the chance.

At least hers had some nice scenery to witness, should they chance a glance out the window in their den. Yes, I'm holding onto that metaphor.

Leila was petite, for lack of a better word, but still shapely. I had an affinity for curves and after getting to know her, I realized they weren't strictly physical. There were no straight lines with Leila, no linearity. She was a smorgasbord of imagination and insanity. My favorite pairing.

These traits were evident in her ink.

Though now mostly covered by hair, she had a black barcode tattoo on her upper nape, the numbers corresponding to her time and date of birth.

Definitely a more creative take than my lower stomach "established" piece.

At least we had some synchronicity going, and that wasn't all.

Leila's left arm, from shoulder to elbow, was a moonlit oceanic tableau. A schooner on the waves, below a large crescent moon encompassing her shoulder, peering down through a cluster of clouds. Beneath the boat, although smaller than the hammerhead on my leg, were a dolphin and mako swimming together, in peace.

In homage to this synchronicity, from the sharks to the moons on our shoulders, we each received a brown-roped anchor on our forearms.

Matching tattoos? Check.

Unashamed lovers of clichés? Check.

Meanwhile, her right arm yielded a multicolored one-eyed owl standing on a blue hourglass, the sand inside red.

The back of her right hand was a basic outline of the U.S., with a yellow blotch in Florida, where she was born, and a red 'X' in South Carolina, where we met.

Adorable, right?

But wait—there's more.

Leila really was a gem, I'm tellin' ya.

Beneath clavicles I'd kissed a thousand times, were tattooed words in black script: *Lusus Naturae*. Latin for "Nature's Freak."

If that brought a smile to your face…

Arching several inches below her navel were more words tattooed in fancy black script.

Latine dici non potest.

"You can't say that in Latin."

She fancied it with a smirk, and deservedly.

During our bedroom escapades—both in and out of the bedroom, mind you—it found its way before my eyes, or beneath my lips, and sometimes I'd come across it…

In other ways.

Always, though, with my own devilish smile.

Oh, Leila.

A lover of Latin—obviously—she originally took up learning it when she was in middle school, as an elective. At first it was merely a piqued curiosity, but it quickly burgeoned into something more. By the time she was twenty, Leila declared that she was fluent in Latin.

And for her, being "fluent in a dead language" was just…undeniably sexy.

Personally, I had to agree.

Along her right thigh was a double-headed rose, with opposing petal coloration—blue and red. Coiling up the thorny stem, unscathed by them, was the outline of a ribbon.

Aside from a pewter anklet, her entire left leg was unadorned.

The Latin inscription on the band read *Facta non Verba*, or "Deeds, Not Words." The irony was clear as day, and delighted her all the more.

Except for a sprawling piece on her back, her only other tattoos were, in fact, unsurprisingly Latin as well. Initially, she had told me, she wanted to get a certain phrase shoulder to shoulder, across her upper back. But she was convinced by a girlfriend at the time to make it more visible. So she opted to break it up, and had them tattooed in the same black script as the others, but in curves—as if the bottoms of hoop earrings—beneath either ear.

Under the left was *fax mentis*, and under the right was *incedium gloriae*. Together they proclaimed "the passion of glory is the torch of the mind."

Goddamn, I loved her.

And she loved me.

So the immense tattoo on her back came to have more meaning than all the others, or so she claimed.

Our anchors matched, but paled in comparison to the companion piece on her exquisite back. A graffiti-styled rendition of the words *SOAKING RED*, with our three-letter initials meshed into it.

"Well?" Leila insisted from the bed, reeling me back into this living dream. She licked her lips and bent a knee, previously parallel thighs now parting. Her hands delicately clawed the sheet in front of her.

A sea of white between us.

I grinned.

"Welcome to the jungle, baby."

II

We fucked like there was no tomorrow. Because for all we knew, there wasn't. And then we fucked some more. It was more a life creed than a sexual mentality, something that sort of governed how we existed together. It was never a matter of teetering at the edge, or predicting consequences and rationalizing decisions.

All-or-nothing, there was no alternative.

It was how we survived day to day, back in "the real world," and it was how we made love, too.

And fucked.

Two sides of the coin. Applicable to both.

We never relented, whether slow songs snake-charmed our bodies in an act of lovemaking, or like gunfire skin slapped skin and teeth gnashed, heralding a raucous climax.

A powerful experience regardless of the circumstances.

Not every instance was perfect.

Over the last two years, we built upon ourselves, improving and evolving as lovers. As partners.

So that each event was memorable, whether a sojourn or an odyssey.

Today, we let the cold stoke our fire, not extinguish it. Her rosy nipples like stalagmites beneath my greedy palms, callused fingers grappling supple breasts, her own hands madly clutching fistfuls of sheets.

Legs parting and closing, wrapping and locking. Prohibiting escape. Demanding depth, surrendering warmth.

We fit together like two puzzle pieces desperate to find a union.

In moments of respite, we didn't connect at all. More rather, we slid and glided. Stroked and kissed, brushed and licked.

There were no motions not admitted.

"Stay," I'd whisper, my mouth obsessed with the journey between her shoulder and neck.

"Follow," she'd gasp, and reluctantly squirm away. The pursuit was fleeting, and impetuous. She seldom folded from my momentum, instead assimilating it. Sometimes the ardor in her kindled a conflagration worth fueling. Our tug-o-wars were never to be taken lightly.

It was only when her hair devolved into reins within my clutches that she succumbed to subdual.

And what a ride that was.

Eventually we changed position, and if it wasn't before, it became clear in that moment: we as humans no longer existed. Our civility had debased into a concept foreign to beasts, replaced by something far more feral. A spectator might so much turn away as be disgusted, or keep watching for the rush.

When we made love, it was a sliver of scenic apple pie anyone would duel to the death for a bite of.

Conversely, when we fucked, like this, it was…an acquired taste, to put simply. More colorfully, I'd compare it to a chunk of granite dropped into a pit of raging lava. The gelatinous heat would eat away at the rock—our inhibitions, or what little remained of them—sans pity or relent. And whatever survived that carnivorous flame was a core that the two of us shared as a whole.

One might argue that it was an orb of genuine, judge-less passion.

To be blunter, we'd state the obvious.

It was the brutal truth, that in such a moment we shared one goal and one goal only.

To get each other off.

At any and all cost.

"Fuck, fuck," she panted, her eyes fierce with lust. Her hips squirming against me, grinding, inviting. My hands cinching the dips in her waist, vice grips until I deemed otherwise.

Once I did, they savored her might.

She was going at her own pace, refusing to pause. A mad bull charging not forward but back, taking me and giving herself in the same radical motion.

Her black hair had gained a sheen from perspiration. Cold as it had become in the room, our breaths pumping visibly, we were still warm-blooded animals, and our love for lust demanded exertion.

I could barely feel the tiny bumps sheeting her skin from nape to coccyx, gooseflesh from the cold. I fleet-ingly wondered if the dripping warmth of my tongue would suppress them.

And then I abandoned thought, taking the advice of a particular anklet inscription. I acted, retracting from her, in an unexpected move. She would have protested had it not been for my tongue, paving a path inside of her from behind.

My eyes peered up, below the summit of her buttocks, hands keeping them spread. Nose buried, raking in her unchaste scent. Fetters shed and wings free, we flew together, hand in hand, lips to lips, as above, so below.

I glimpsed her head whip back, hair fluttering above her shoulder blades. A wet gasp like a melting dagger cutting the air.

Whether or not an invitation, I saw what I wanted to, and knew that in the end, she would thank me.

As I ascended behind her, though, those delicious moans sputtered to a sudden stop, and she leered back at me with ambivalence. I could only grin diabolically, my manhood gliding between her thumbprint dimples of Venus. Simultaneously, I ran a solitary finger up her back, from base camp to peak, partially tracing her *SOAKING RED* tattoo, ultimately pausing at her nape.

I formed a wide U with my hand, gently but firmly gripping the back of her neck. Her stare mutated into a grin, and she turned her head to look forward. I then collapsed my hand and slid it up through her hair, guiding her head down, bowing between her outstretched arms.

She lifted her back end against me, and chills swept through my loins.

My eyelids fluttered briefly.

I smirked, and then lowered my face to the side of hers, nuzzling through black curtains of hair. My voice slinked into her right ear.

"Here, my love," I said, quietly, as if conducting espionage. "Lie down here."

She practically collapsed beneath me, but in a far

more graceful manner. Her toes extended, heels out and knees together, between my feet. Out of sight. My mind, and everything else, fixated on something far more treasured to me.

As I guided myself into her tepid delta, I saw my breath manifest before me. All thanks to this cold, and I of course couldn't complain. Thanks to this cold, we were both sculptures of ice and stone with embers pulsing inside of us, warming our veins and granting us the sustenance of motion.

Thanks to this cold, I was still going at it.

And running on way more than fumes, I'd have you know.

A gentle yet unforgiving plunge inside, from behind, and I was reminding Leila she was still alive. The feeling was mutual; a sensation that might warrant a contemplation on what it meant to be human, if we weren't so mindless in the act.

She released a deep moaning sound, guttural at first. Not unlike a panther's throaty growl, fending off any threat. The situation was different, however—no threat here. Just the two of us, sodden with passion.

Soaking red.

"Where do you want it?" I murmured, leaning forward and hovering over her head. My voice floated through the cold and snaked into her skull.

Squirming beneath me, she paused to turn her head and bless me with a profile view of her breathtaking face. Not a speck of makeup, just the raw beauty of her submission to pleasure.

Her lips were ajar, albeit not spewing moans. Her

brow was furrowed, that bittersweet emotion overwhelming her once more.

"Inside," she muttered, music in two syllables.

I planted a wet kiss on her cheek, and then slid a pair of fingers into her mouth. She treated them like a saccharine candy, the panacea to her sweet tooth. Meanwhile I grinded against her prone figure, probing her velvety, saturated lair betwixt tremulous thighs.

She moaned little squeals around my fingers, and I delighted at the sight of her eyelids fluttering.

"Come on, now," I said, as if she was being too gluttonous.

Part of my mouth warped into a sinister grin as I withdrew my fingers, saliva roping after them, and then guided my hand down, around her right ribcage. My thighs straddled her hips, and then squeezed to lift. The rest was history.

I reached between her and the damp sheets.

"Oh my fucking—" Leila's voice broke.

It was a beautifully chaotic dispersion of sound. I savored every distorted syllable, every lilting breath that came crashing through her lips.

Her body writhed beneath me, my hips driving once more, and my hand—those two fingers previously in her mouth but now wetter than ever—thriving inside.

Eventually her name broke my lips, in a lovely mess. As her body undulated beneath, and against, mine, she reciprocated that same expression. My name staggered out of her mouth, for "Lucas" and "Leila" were the only valid words in the heat of such a moment. Anything else, save for a myriad variations of "fuck," just didn't suffice.

Except for maybe a shrill "I'm gonna—"

And then we did. A seemingly simultaneous climax. First the deluge, and then the storm. As I filled my love, her skies fell around me.

A mutual warmth, to top everything that had preceded it.

Inexplicably content, we basked in the aftermath of our rugged bliss, somehow still sweating despite the icy ends of our fingertips, chins, and earlobes.

I breathed into her ear, lying atop her with an ounce of restraint, and watched the air billow around her face. She smiled and turned onto her side, allowing my body to slide down beside her and gaze into those stunning brown gems.

"How long?" She exhaled calmly.

I shrugged, lips pursed, and she immediately smiled. A microscopic expression, not gone unnoticed. Her every smallest feature or reaction was always worthy of vast scrutiny.

I parted a tress of her black hair with my hand, curling it behind an ear. It had been sticking to her cheek from the perspiration.

"Five to ten," I responded quietly.

Her previously infinitesimal smile now dilated into something wonderfully wider. I smirked myself, unable to resist it at the sight of her grinning. Simultaneously, my left hand sashayed down the valley of her waist and hips.

"What about you?" I asked.

"What do you mean, 'what about me'?" She replied, failing to repress a giggle.

"Alright, alright," I grinned, and rolled onto my back.

I raked in a deep breath, hands on my remotely hair-stippled chest. I watched a pillar of breath climb through the air above me, and then turned my head to look at her. She was smiling, toothlessly now, just looking at me. Her right hand crept closer, fingers tapping on my chest. I touched her hand, caressing her white knuckles, and then spoke. "Would you mind shutting that window, though?"

"Oh," she said, eyebrows hiking. "So you want it slow, do you?"

I shrugged, still supine.

"I still want it soaking, but, yes…"

Leila grinned and withdrew her hand, rolling away in the same motion. Her hair, like a militia of black mambas, slithered after her, as she gracefully dismounted the bed.

For a moment she was a blur of pale skin and vibrant ink. The pinkness of her lips, nipples, and the spots on her butt from our colliding bodies were barely discernible— yet far from unremarkable.

Leila stood in front of the window, between the wall and that side of the bed. From behind, she was almost as gorgeous as she was facing me. My eyes crept up her calves to the backside of her thighs, and then hovered over the curvature of her lower body. With a self-satisfied sigh, my gaze continued its gluttonous ascent, slowly drifting over her tattooed back.

The *SOAKING RED* graffiti had made her skin an opus to our names.

I remembered how Leila had come up with the phrase. We were lying in bed, after making love for the longest duration in our relationship. We had barely been a year in at that point, but what a fucking year.

That particular evening I could recall every single detail.

Sheets were as if draped over an Amazonian branch, white and sodden. Our bodies clammy and slick with sweat, gleaming in lamplight and the pressing glow of dusk through curtains. Strands of her especially long black hair clung to her face, like strips of onyx. Her eyes were nothing short of bedazzling.

We were in the midst of catching our breaths.

This wasn't at the cabin, no. It had been at my place, and to have *had* her like that in my own bed was something inexplicably euphoric. It only intensified the significance of how much we loved each other, and I could see it in her eyes, that she felt the same.

We lolled there like two sloths after mating all day, reveling in our own carnal glory.

Leila was on her side, her body snugly parallel to mine. With a cheek on my chest, she breathed me in and crept a finger down my stomach, my arm, and back up again.

"You're soaked in it," she whispered.

"Hmm?" I asked, raising an eyebrow and tilting my head to get a better view of her face.

"Red with passion," she said, her voice soft and velveteen. She looked up at me. "You're soaking red with it. You're aglow."

I smiled, and parted the hair clinging to her cheek. I then massaged the earlobe beneath where I tucked the hair, with my thumb and forefinger.

"I'll take that as a compliment," I said, feeling pleasantly speechless in that moment.

And many more to come.

I leaned in to kiss her, and our lips joined for the longest breath. When we reclined again, she started gently kissing my chest. With my right arm under her neck and across her back, I rested my hand beneath her right breast. Even clammy with sweat, her skin was impeccably soft.

"If I'm soaking," I added, drinking in the sight of her with more than my eyes, "then you're exploding with it."

Gradually, the pair of words became a sort of sensual motto, and mantra, between us. It defined us as a couple, our relationship both in and out of bed. Red was the ubiquitous color of passion, the hue of heat, and seemingly everything we did was saturated with it.

Roughly four months following that night, we planned out the shared tattoos. Adding our initials was my idea, and with her help we designed the layout ourselves. We were, afterall, both artists. I was the poet, for lack of a better word, and she the painter. I would beg to differ that I was as much an artist as her, for she truly had talent with a brush.

Masterpieces could be birthed from the most rugged, blank canvases, at her hand.

And so she created one with her back. Given, we attended a professional tattoo artist, but the design was ours, and I'd argue mostly hers.

Imperfect as our bodies were, I'd never stop dramatizing the immaculacy of hers. But she saw her previously untouched back as a canvas that needed a lick of art, and a symbol of purpose. The *SOAKING RED* graffiti became both, and she would swear by it.

Smooth and seemingly unblemished as her back had been, Leila often saw it as the bearer of her troubles over the years. First carried by her shoulders, only to drip down and scar invisibly.

We both had been through so much, even so young.

With a slam, Leila shut the window.

"Better?" She asked, her voice of silk. With a turn on her heel, she refaced me and the bed.

By god, she was both ghost and goddess in my eyes.

With a model's strut, she strode toward the bed, her ankles crossing and her thighs hugging. My stare crawled up her groin, her pierced navel, her smooth breasts, and her light cerise lips. She poked her tongue out briefly, licked them, and then raised a brow.

"Much better," I smirked, and beckoned her.

Leila climbed onto the bed, crawling on all fours toward me. The mattress was stubbornly stiff, not unlike my current revived state, but we put it to use. As she would me.

When she reached me, no words were exchanged at first. Only the damp sounds of lips pressing, and coalescing. There was beauty and delight to the supple chaos, though, as our lips intermittently missed their mark. Once they locked, however, it was our tongues' time to join in on the lovely disorder. Two serpents unsure of where to go and what to do, entangled in a confusion. Wrestling and investigating all at once, in a pair of caged mouths.

One of my hands found its way to her face, cupping a cheek and caressing an earlobe.

I heard and felt her exhale into my mouth.

Two syllables carrying with it.

"Soaking," she murmured in that delectable breath. And before I could respond, she withdrew to lie on her back before me. I watched her practically plummet from my grasp, in slow motion, when in reality she merely slumped back onto the bed, a cobra being tamed into its basket. The sheets fluttered around her figure, the residual cold in the room drying previously damp fabric. In addition to the sheets, her tattoos accentuated her slim yet shapely figure

I hovered over her, positioning.

A soft kiss landed on her neck, and her body outstretched beneath me, knees locking and toes pointing like a ballet dancer.

"Red," I whispered, slowly entering.

We shared a kiss as I dove deeper.

Memories flooded my mind of times past. Similar but disparate. Not one identical to the other.

Our stomachs grazed and we breathed into each other's mouths. Lips touched and tongues grappled. My hands turned to fists and they bore down into the mattress on either side of Leila's shoulders. They propped me up, pillars to my roof. My pelvis was fueled by my fervor, my desire, my yearning and my love.

I thrusted and she grinded, our bodies moving in unison. Any clumsiness moments ago was discarded and forgotten, like shed snakeskin. We evolved and devolved at the same time, into something simpler and more transparent.

We undulated as one.

"Yes, yes," she panted, breaths sharp and raspy.

I clenched my jaw and bared my teeth to her. With

each thrust I gave in faster and harder, striving deeper and stronger. Her body shuddered beneath me, her face distorted with pleasure and hunger.

Her insides tightened around me, throbbing and seeping.

The sensation was incomparable, and difficult to paint with words. Had I felt it earlier, when we were fucking like unholy beasts?

How could I not have?

This time was different, though. Somehow it seemed bolder, and heavier. Our intimacy, that face-to-face privacy, was unrivaled.

I lowered myself to her, closer. Our lips skimmed in rhythm with my thrusts, never fully clasping. Our bellies grazed again. Her hands flew up from beneath the pillow, where they had been hiding, and latched onto my back. Conservative fingernails finding purchase in my skin. There was no blood drawn; they were merely anchors, and incentives.

It was an action that had become routine between us. It was her wordless way of demanding I not relent. No matter what.

Fuck drawing it out, or tempting the fall.

So I went faster. Yielding to nothing.

And yet, somehow or another, we were still going slower than before. Which wasn't to say we were even going slow. It was an incalculable speed, the rate in which we fucked and how we made love.

Perhaps it was all in my mind.

Perhaps I thought too much.

In reality, there was no mulling it over. It was all in

the heat of the instant, seconds dripping into minutes. We had pushed ourselves close to an hour in the past, on more than one occasion. But, in addition to the cold, other factors were present. A plan, a strategy, and the patience to draw back when at other times we'd simply crash forward like waves at the command of a full moon.

Today it was so very different.

We acted on a whim, obeying only each other's gestures and instincts.

She wasn't the only one subdued. I had submitted the second I laid eyes on her.

"Yes!" She wailed, her head jerking back, hoisting her shoulders off the bed.

My hands found the base of her neck as I drove myself to the hilt, and bathed in a peaking warmth below. I witnessed her shudder beneath me, feeling every square inch of her tremor ecstatically.

Descending upon her, I turned my lips into a stamping machine, kissing her rapidly from breasts to mouth.

Leila's breaths became choppy from exhaustion, patiently recovering from her orgasm. I decelerated to savor it as well, until I ceased motion altogether, floating above her.

When our eyes connected again, her right hand touched my face. Cupped my cheek, and rubbed a gauged earlobe. Then her other hand vanished down between us, until it located what she blindly sought. Her hands were still a bit cold from earlier, and I reflexively flinched from her touch.

She giggled and I kissed the sound from her mouth.

At the same time, her hand guided me back inside,

and her mouth slackened beneath me. A delicious expression.

Her hands surfaced to the sheets, where she held them at either side of her shoulders, offering herself. A gentle smile swept her face.

"C'mere," I whispered, and leaned back with my legs tucked under me, knees in the mattress. She hoisted herself up, too, and spread her legs. Her feet passed by my hips, so that her thighs hugged my pelvis, and I wrapped both arms behind her, cradling.

In the same fluid motion, which I recalled being a clumsy mess the first and second time we tried it, I reentered her. There was only an impure gracefulness this instance.

We held each other in a reciprocal hug, warmer than before. Lips mashing and eventually hands mating, fingers interlocking.

It was a wonder we didn't have magnets in our chests.

The embrace was short-lived, although in our minds and hearts it was worthy of eternity.

When we separated, we still came together, though it was I who erupted this time. Details aside, a shower would certainly have to follow.

Which had already been assumed.

And of course, it would be together.

Seldom were our showers not, if we had control of the situation.

Here, we were gods of our own paths.

With deep respirations, we lied back down. Leila on her back, and I rolled over next to her. When I looked at her, she was smiling, peering up at the drab ceiling.

"I sure do hope that's a smile of satisfaction," I couldn't help but say.

"When is it not?" She replied, and turned her head to look at me, a faint glint in her dark eyes.

"Touché," I said, smirking.

"How 'bout we go out, after a shower?" She proposed, eyebrows raised.

"Define *out*."

"Out*side*, ya know?" She said, matter-of-factly. And then simpered. "Frolic."

I laughed. "You wanna take a shower, and *then* 'frolic'?"

"Why not?" She shrugged, playfully scowling at first. Then she shrugged. "Besides, it's not like we can take too many showers."

I nodded, mulling over how right she was.

The cabin's water supply was a drilled well whose resource was a local spring. Weekly, it was monitored and maintained by the people responsible for renting out the cabin, and contributed to the cost, along with the septic system and generator.

We just got here two days ago, and still had the rest of the week all to ourselves. With, of course, the surrounding wilderness to witness our antics. We both wished we could stay longer, but the cabin was no cheap expense, and neither of us were exactly loaded. Besides, "the real world" still existed back home, and certain responsibilities never truly died, they only took vacation.

The cabin itself was no exquisite mansion, and only

one story, but the efficiency of utilities and isolation demanded cost.

"How about we snag something to eat before we head out?" I suggested. "After the shower."

"Sounds good to me," she said, nuzzling me briefly before a big smile foreshadowed her departure. She rolled off the bed, onto her bare feet, and stood up straight. The floorboards creaked gently beneath her. "I'm gonna go…rinse off. You can join me in a few."

I watched her trot toward the bathroom, if that was even an accurate term, given the floorplan.

Whoever designed this cabin must have been on drugs. And once the blueprints were submitted, nobody really cared. Hell, we certainly didn't, beyond a joke or two. It was peculiar, but not unbearable.

With Leila as company, I barely even noticed.

III

Showering with your partner was usually more exhilarating in mind than in reality. Sometimes even embarrassing, with the potential for a myriad of awkward moments. I certainly had my fair share of them with past girlfriends. Of course, none of them could even remotely compare to what Leila and I shared. Sure, we had our own awkward exchanges, but they were never mortifying. If anything, they concreted our bond, and reminded us of our humanity.

We had nothing to hide from each other, nothing to be ashamed of, and that went for our pasts, too.

Back to the shower.

Given the intensity of our sessions, even we were surprised of our cold bodies afterward. With the frigid climate outside, and the halfway-decent heating in the cabin, there was a mild limbo of temperature always creeping through. It made sleeping at night perfect, especially snuggled together, but after having the window open for so long during our collision of flesh, some of it stayed with us.

Bottom line, we would enjoy a lukewarm shower. Leila was already ahead of me, too, doing just that. When I traipsed into view of the stall shower, sliding glass door wide open, all I could do for the longest instant was stare.

Her back arched slightly, arms raised and hands lathering conditioner into her hair. The coconut scent titillated me almost as much as the sight of her did. Even with particular features of her nude body veiled by suds.

By the time she turned ever so slightly to glimpse me ogling her, I was itching to go again. Any tiredness of my virile youth be damned.

I swapped smiles with her, and approached.

She sidestepped beneath the angled showerhead, rinsing her hair and body, soap washing away in thick cascades of opaque water.

I entered the stall and slid the glass door shut behind me. It wasn't the quietest motion on its steel rails, but the natural music of water pattering the tile upon which we stood, and coursing over Leila's body, was louder.

Beneath the showerhead I stepped, molding my limbs and body to hers. Sharing the halo of descending water. Warm but leagues from hot, or cold. Just right.

We kissed between curtains of water, falling from our brows.

In the shower, no mess could be made.

I lowered a hand and slapped her buttocks, slinging water onto the glass and tile around us. She giggled and water bubbled from her lips. Seconds melted into minutes as we stood there, idly dancing with each other, particularly her against me. We became a pair of dysfunctional scissors set out in a monsoon, gentle as one could ever be, careless if we were to rust. Or in this case, prune.

Not the first occurrence we would lose track of time in the shower.

At least we didn't forget to wash, which had happened before. With Leila, it was easy to forget even the most basic of things.

It was, however, rushed. Because other deeds called for greater urgency. I could have waited, but Leila would not be made to if she had anything to say about it.

Ultimately, we ended up fucking again.

Or did we make love?

Admittedly, it was a challenge to differentiate in the shower. We would have these moments where she likened herself to a Greek statue before me, though one infused with vitalism, nonetheless at the mercy of my hands and…divining rod.

I'd seize her and unleash myself in waves of wanton lust that might never be forgiven.

Her wails, siren song aching to witness my shipwreck on her silken rocks.

Even still, I would hoist her up and hold her in hopes she would melt into me, slowly, despite the raging waters we had just embodied.

And in that instant, fleeting or otherwise, nothing else fucking mattered.

Nothing.

The world could be crumbling all around us, angels weeping and falling from butchered skies, hell rising up from massive fissures in the earth, atmosphere charring like battery acid.

Any and everything and nothing at all.

We were undisturbed for that stretch of heartbeats, sharing the serenity in our adjoined flesh.

Yet when we resumed, it was all of those violent things and more, harnessed into our own bodies.

It ended with a cry out of shattering pleasure, a sound that escaped Leila's mouth unlike anything ever documented. It was beautiful and in itself arousing, enough to make me stop teetering and give in to the fall, myself.

Any remaining suds were washed away, and whatever mess had been made was dispensed of as if by a natural rain.

The pipes in the wall creaked like age-old creatures being woken from a decade's slumber. They weren't very happy about it, either. I cringed from the sound, quite a contrast to the chaotic melodies Leila had made.

When the faucet cut off, the echoes inside the walls faded.

"Maybe we oughtta shower outside, next time," I suggested, half-serious. It wasn't like we couldn't; there was a crank-shower system out the back door.

I exited the stall and snagged a towel from the rack on the wall. As I began drying myself off, Leila followed suit, starting with her drenched hair.

"To be honest," she said, "I'd be down for that. And I love the cold and everything…but not this time of year. Maybe August or September."

"Yeah," I smirked. "That would be nice."

"Especially out here," she said, pensively, a delicate smile on her face. "The woods surrounding us, the birds chirping and all the critters."

"You can be weird sometimes, ya know?" I joked, one eyebrow raised.

Leila grinned and shook her head. After her hair, she buried her face in the towel, then moved it down her neck and chest. I shamelessly became a little enrapt with her drying off, a routine and menial task but because it was Leila, felt like a drug.

Once we were both dried off, we flung the towels over our shoulders. No need for privacy here.

But of course, Leila's hair would remain damp for some time after.

"So how far do you wanna go?" She asked, gesturing at a wall.

"All the way," I answered with a straight face. She passed in front of me and rolled her eyes. I just as playfully smacked her butt only to lean in to steal a kiss of her neck. She gave in to a smile and we came so close to doing the dirty yet again.

This time, though, it was me who pulled away.

"Too tired for another round?" She teased.

"Psh, nah," I shook my head. Then I pulled in close to her, as she opened a clothes drawer. I hooked an arm around her waist and pressed myself against her bare body. A few beads of water still clung to our skin, here and there, only then rubbing into oblivion. "It's never about the fatigue, Leila. It's about what *we* wanna do. And I know you wanna go outside, so I'm all in. As for how far…" I shrugged. "However far nature takes us."

We shared a tacit smile and settled with that.

The cabin offered two separate dressers, one smaller than the other. Inside, unless we were really cold or bugs had invaded, Leila and I seldom wore proper clothes. The scantier the better.

Anytime we ventured outside, however, layers were intrinsic. So, over boxers, I slipped on a pair of jeans and two shirts, then a hooded sweater. We each brought with us a very limited wardrobe, given our propensity for near-nudity, and the seven-day stay.

Even Leila gave in to this, with a minor exception. She of course had brought a few more articles of clothing than I had, albeit nothing outrageous. I respected that she had fashion sense where I had little to none. At least she was self-aware about where we were.

The middle of a Tennessean forest, not downtown Miami.

Long story short, to no surprise, Leila had dibs on the larger dresser. A mahogany vanity, dwarfing my oak dresser, which was without a mirror. The paint was chipping and the drawers squeaked whenever pulled out. Leila's, on the other hand, was next to pristine. And best believe she made great use of its tall, ovoid mirror.

Once I was dressed, I turned to face Leila. She was still in front of the vanity, pulling her jeans on. I relished her passing struggle to squeeze herself into the denim, thus concealing a meager pair of black panties beneath.

She had yet to put her bra on, supposing she would choose to wear one.

"I'm gonna go ahead and make breakfast, babe," I told her, passing by.

"Oh, okay," she nodded. A moment later: "So…what are you gonna make? Cereal?" A punctual giggle.

"Ha-ha," I said ironically. "And no. You'll just have to wait 'n' see."

"Oh, dear, the suspense is *killing* me," she said theatrically, only to roll her eyes like brown marbles while the corners of her mouth curled into the faintest smile.

Her hands proceeded to rummage through a variety of tops in an upper drawer.

"Enjoy it," I teased her, grinning, and exited the room.

I all but marched, confidently, into the kitchen. Just around a corner, only part of it visible from the bed, if the door was left open.

That's right, folks. Lucas Bravo was going to make his girl breakfast. Cereal? Couldn't say I didn't consider it. Instead, I hit up the refrigerator as if it was a bank that desperately needed robbing. I fetched four eggs and a jug of milk. Then I spun on my heel to dig through a cupboard, ultimately snatching a carton of microwaveable grits.

Next, the necessary utensils from the freshly furnished drawers.

I turned the gas stove on and let the range heat up. Silverware, plates, napkins, and two glasses were next.

Lo and behold, I was getting ahead of myself.

I paused to retrieve what some might consider the most essential item of such a traditionally American breakfast.

Bacon.

Straight from the freezer, I unpackaged it and striped the large pan with eight strips. As soon as they started to sizzle, I trashed the tray, wanting to appear fully in control of the situation. And I was. Leila knew I was no

Bobby Flay, but I could hold the fort down in the kitchen, without setting the house on fire, if it came to that.

More than anything I just wanted to provide for her after today's buffet of deviant acts in the bedroom. So many that at this point it was actually early afternoon instead of morning.

Given, I already had "provided" in more ways than one, but she knew how much I revered her—even out of the bedroom.

And everybody loved bacon.

Besides, I was famished.

Sure, I *had* just eaten, but not food.

"Damn, that smells good," Leila said, her voice and gaze slick. Her nostrils flared and she closed her eyes briefly, taking it in. "Ah, bacon."

"Just started, so it'll be a bit."

"No worries," she said, kissing my right cheek, and then standing off to the side, elbow on the counter. I could feel her eyes on me, as opposed to what I was doing; never not a pleasant thing. "And what else, Mr. Ramsay?"

"Eggs and grits." I paused to glance at her. "Sorry, Leila, no Cheerios. Maybe tomorrow."

"Oh, well," she said, suppressing a smile. "Maybe it'll actually be morning then, too."

We caved to share a small laugh.

"Yeah, we kinda got carried away, didn't we?" I said, returning my attention to the preparation of grits.

"Nothing bad about that," she smirked. "A due workout, too. And I'm just *loving* this isolation."

"Amen to that."

"Separation from the real world and all its stupid bullshit," she added, taking a deep breath before smiling contentedly. "Just you and I, and love, and nature."

"Paradise," I said, briefly pensive.

I heard Leila giggle before suddenly reaching out and tapping an egg I had set on the counter. It swiftly rolled off the edge of the counter, into the sink. I caught it before it splatted against the stainless steel.

"You devil," I said, head turned and a corner of my mouth curled up.

She shrugged and snickered.

"Just keeping the cook on his toes," she smiled.

I cracked the one I had caught, smoothly, and then dumped the yolk into a measuring glass.

"How many do you want, *princess*?"

"Just one's fine. I think I'll pig out on the bacon."

"Touché."

After getting the eggs in the pan and the grits in the microwave, whisk in hand to stir the yolks, I felt a pair of arms curl around my waist. Fingers interlaced and Leila's body pressed against my back, her head turned, face nuzzled between my shoulder blades. I reached down with a free hand and caressed her knuckles, relishing how they had warmed since the shower.

I tilted my head back, stretching at the same time, and she kissed my nape.

Usually this was all reversed, and I was the one behind her. But she had taken me by pleasant surprise.

I paused from the eggs to half-turn and align my lips with hers. She was right there to meet me, so a brief kiss was shared.

"Is this how you wish to do me in?" I asked quietly, the sizzling of bacon and eggs and the running of the microwave to our right all a background symphony. "Hug me from behind, distract me with those lips, and then *push* me into the gas stove?"

"No, of course not," she said. A pause. "But you have to admit…it wouldn't be a terrible way to go. Aside from the burning, you'd get a face-full of bacon *and* eggs…putting a whole new twist on *last supper*."

Our veneers dissolved and we shared a chuckle or two.

Then Leila unhooked herself and I hastily shifted gears to keep the food from blackening. Knobs turned the stove off and I transitioned pans to unused burners. Cheers to great timing, the microwave went off. I stepped over to remove the bubbling grits, while Leila poured milk into two glasses, plinking an ice cube from the freezer in each.

She returned the gallon to the fridge, already half-empty, but we had two whole quarts in the back as reserve.

"Strong bones for strong lovers," I had joked before, at our shared fondness of milk.

With everything prepared, Leila serving the grits and I dishing out the rest, we "set the table." Except there was none. The kitchen had two countertops, one against the wall, shared by the sink and refrigerator, and an island behind it, on top of cabinets. The other side of the island stood wooden barstools, which we perched on to use the narrow counter as a makeshift table.

"Not bad, Lucas," she said after scarfing down her eggs and beginning on her bacon, separately.

"Why thank you, my love," I said, a little theatrically, and then downed half of my milk in one voracious swig.

You know how you know you truly love someone? When eating a meal—something as trite as just another breakfast or lunch—and you shared eye contact that surpassed words. It didn't have to be Thanksgiving dinner or the last meal of the year, waiting for that ball to drop in Times Square, champagne glasses within reach. No, you were sitting on the couch or at a rickety table in your crappy little house spooning Frosted Flakes like a little kid, embracing the unseen emotions that the eyes of two lovers shared.

That was one way to truly know.

Of course, if you were indubitably in love and certain that nothing could deviate it but death—if even that— then you didn't need proof.

You just knew.

"I'll take care of the dishes, you go on and head outside," Leila said once we had finished, not far apart from each other.

"No, it's okay, I'll—"

"I've *got it*," she insisted, leering.

I laughed. "Okay, okay. I'll get the porch, grass, and trees ready for you. Nature won't know what hit 'em. But *I* will, and I'll love every bit of it."

I winked at her for the hell of it and she smiled and waved me off.

I hit the bathroom first, brushing my teeth and catching another glimpse of myself in that sooty mirror. This time it was far more transient, and less ambivalent. I saw the gratitude in my eyes and face that I felt whenever I shared a breath with Leila. I saw it, and I embraced the humility.

Then I headed out, glancing at Leila in the kitchen, her back turned, en route to the front door. I slipped my sneakers on and stuffed both hands in the pockets of my sweater, hood down, before exiting the cabin. I left the front door open, the heavy wood squeaking on its hinges, and closed the screen.

I took a deep breath before watching it billow out before me.

The natural light from the cloudless sky was beautiful and perfect, especially when perceived through the tops of thinning canopies.

In front of the wooden porch was a large patch of gravel, though no vehicles nearby. Desiring utter isolation, not to mention a different sort of road trip for once, we hitched our way up here.

With the cabin already rented for the week, we only had to adhere to a time frame. Once in the area, we had the option to rent an ATV, and being the gearhead I was, I nearly flew off the handle about it. But after minimal consideration, I knew it wasn't necessary. If anything, it could potentially ruin our time together.

What good was absolute isolation and tranquility if there was one more thing reminding you that the world still existed and it was roaring through the calm forest just for the sake of getting from Point A to Point B faster than walking?

I could easily live without it.

Even with Leila insisting that it was alright just to settle my nerves on the matter, I ultimately buckled down and said the two key words to any dilemma.

"Fuck it."

Given, they could be plugged into virtually any situation, good or bad.

Leila wasn't foreign to its use, either.

Which was another reason why we got along so famously.

The cabin rested on a small knoll, so the front yard was actually a slight slope that descended just past the strip of gravel. Beyond it were tame grasses and some taller weeds the closer you got to an encircling treeline.

The wilderness itself.

The surrounding woods were terrifically vast. It could be seen as one large, sentient beast that sustained its privacy so long as it wasn't too incredibly disturbed.

We had only been here for two days, but the deer and raccoons had made themselves known to us. The latter would make a ruckus at night, whenever they pleased, so long as the sun was down. In the late evening we could hear their little claws skitter across the porch, likely searching for a way in or something else to feast on. Nothing sufficient to keep us awake, nor much of an annoyance. If anything, we occasionally got a chuckle at out of it.

Leila and I were heavy sleepers, anyway, especially given such detachment from "real life."

No matter what, though, Leila was a brick of a sleeper, whereas I usually took a few minutes to actually fall asleep.

Fortunately we had not experienced any run-ins with wolves or bears, nor any sightings, since we arrived. Only when we first got here did we venture out, like we were preparing to do now; we did so first-thing, leaving our belongings on the porch. It was a kind of wake-up call, an acknowledgment of how far out we had come, and how alone we were.

The walk had been a meditation of sorts.

It ended with dusk creeping to an end, and we got to witness the sunset just over the treetops. An orange-yellow eye victimized by exhaustion, yet no less beautiful than at its brightest.

At its darkest hour, the sun was most alluring.

Leila would agree.

After everything we had been through, individually, it seemed there was something redeeming about that. Seeing the beauty in darkness, the enduring light where shadow reigned.

Hands still in my hoodie's pockets, I trudged down the porch steps, until my shoes crunched gravel. I walked to the edge, where the grassy slope peaked, and then paused. I turned to my right, where a natural trail led away from the cabin, at a steadier incline than the one straight down the front. Where the trail ventured into the woods, it was widest, nearly twelve feet. Less than ten paces in, however, it tapered as it snaked farther into the forest, its path appearing overgrown the deeper it went.

When Leila and I first walked off those two days ago, we hadn't gone far. Just enough to catch a nice angle of the sun descending over, and through, thinning canopies.

We could very well have continued. The trail led downhill from where we stopped, over a small wooden bridge and more into the forest than any footpath might.

Sometimes I was surprised at how long she and I could go before tiring. Whether it was walking, staying up late, or going at it in the bedroom. She had joked just the other day that we had built nerves of steel from countless sessions of lovemaking, fucking, exercising, hiking, and losing our minds to loud music.

I of course saw the truth in the joke.

And with the absence of drugs in our lives, we equally loved mellowing out to pensive music, too. The company shared was often enough to usher interesting conversations and astral sensations.

That evening we wandered away from the cabin, for once there was some ration left in our minds. Given the encroaching darkness and our unfamiliarity with these woods, we chose not to push our luck and headed back.

Besides, the sunset had more than sufficed.

I looked up, away from the trail. There was no tree-cover above the cabin and its little knoll. A lovely spot in the dense forestry surrounding it.

No clouds at the moment, and the sun shone unabashedly.

Perhaps today we could walk a little farther than that evening. Sightsee birds and possums, or just the trees and foliage, thick as it was around here. Maybe there was even a creek nearby, possibly by the small bridge we spotted earlier.

That would be nice.

I didn't wander too far, just off the gravel and a few paces toward the aforementioned trail. Still well within view of the cabin's front door. I wouldn't dream of doing any adventuring without Leila by my side.

"I'm coming, just a minute!" I heard her voice call to me through the screen door.

Once Leila was out of the cabin, closing both doors behind her, she trotted down the porch steps and across the gravel, with haste. Her black and white Vans kept her afoot, those lean yet toned legs clad in denim, graceful when they needed to be and yet adorably clumsy at other times. A smile burgeoned on my face as I watched her shuffle to my side, wearing a black Drop Dead varsity jacket with lime-green trim.

She was dark and flashy all at once, my Leila.

Beneath the jacket, who could say, but she looked warm and comfortable.

"Sorry," she said, briefly baring her teeth. "Got to the door only to realize I wasn't wearing socks."

"Smooth move," I smiled.

She smirked and playfully elbowed me.

"So, Columbus, where we headed?"

I shrugged. "Dunno. Just walk the same trail as before, 'til you wanna head back?"

"Sounds like a plan."

She swung her hips and bumped into mine. I acted as if she was the Hulk and staggered off to the side, arms flailing. I damn near tripped myself in the façade.

"Stop fuckin' around," she laughed.

Grinning, I returned to her side. We locked arms and ambled down the trail, side-by-side.

Two flirtatious tourists of the wild, with nothing tying us down, we trekked without a care in the world as to how we might be perceived.

Every now and then Leila would break our arm link and strut ahead of me, teasing with her stride and the view I was blessed with. Some might argue that the skintight jeans were complementing her, but I'd say that her form complemented the denim. Regardless, I'd eventually jog to catch up and give her a good slap where it counted. She'd chirp and then giggle as I proceeded to mimic her same walk, not sparing any amount of femininity.

Ultimately she would wolf-whistle, as if I had the same goods she had, and was just as irresistible.

I respected Leila's opinion about everything, but when it came to us, she was a little biased and I'd hand her that. However, I'd still argue that she was leagues more attractive than me. Sure, I was a handsome fella, but at the weigh-in she'd easily turn more heads, men and women alike.

We weren't perfect, of course…

But Leila was pretty damn close.

Walking this trail of ours—nay, of the forest's—was fun in itself. The gathering of trees voyeuristically watching us as we strode between them. They were bare trunks and leafy limbs still alive in the peak of autumn. The tallgrass and weeds lining the trail were like fences to us. They tacitly forbade us to cross them, unless a path was already made.

Whether or not we would respect this implication, time and impulses could only tell.

For the moment, however, we did.

Which was why we finally decided to cross that small wooden bridge we had only glimpsed two nights ago. The hill down to it was rather steep, deeply rooted in the middle of the trail by unseen trees, their reach stubborn and perilous but not unpleasant to the eye. The roots themselves, and how they gouged the earth, were gnarled and seemingly ageless. It was a sight that might have gone unnoticed by most, but Leila and I lapped it up. Given, we were also mindful of our step, for the sake of our own safety.

"You sure you wanna go?" I asked Leila, helping her down without tripping. It was a mutual exchange of stability.

"Yeah, why not?" Our eyes met, her gentle hand in my callused grip. Her voice always a delight to hear, no matter the tone. "I mean, fuck it. It's nice out here. And it's so clear outside."

"You read my mind, babe," I said and we descended the hill without much difficulty.

The bridge itself was just ten feet across and maybe six down. One could hardly call it a creek, the stream which it crossed over. Just shallow brown water, with muddy banks and no fish to speak of.

Not the most appealing sight, but the bridge was quaint and could be appreciated.

"At least it's sturdy," Leila said, looking over at me while we crossed it.

"Say that now, and on the way back it collapses," I said in my serious voice.

"Don't say that!" Leila scowled, half-grinning and clocking me in the shoulder.

I winced, melodramatically.

Then I took my reaction a step further.

"Do that again and it won't have to break, you'll have shoved me over the railing!"

"Oh, boohoo, I'm sure you could take it."

"I honestly don't *know*, Leila! Have you even looked over the side? It's at least ten feet deep of shit-creek water down there."

"What? No way," she pshawed.

"No, but seriously," I said, nearly all the way across, throwing on my solemn face. "Take a look. Just hold onto the guardrail."

The railing was wood, too, composed of two horizontal planks about a foot apart from each other. I was almost positive Leila saw the stream earlier, through the underbrush shrouding the banks, and just how shallow the water really was. Let alone how minor such a drop would be. Still, she fell for my trickery—whether intentionally or not, I couldn't be sure, but didn't care.

She turned to peer over the side, palms hugging the top plank and chest pressing against her knuckles.

She leaned forward, looking down.

I moved in behind her, slipping an arm between her legs and the other around her stomach, then lifted.

To throw her over the edge.

All an act. I wasn't letting her go anywhere.

"Oh my god, let me down!" She screeched, knowing I was playing with her but flailing anyways. She started slapping my arms and back even as I set her down—on the ground, having crossed the bridge.

The trail extending behind her was even more beautiful than the one we had taken to get here. The overlapping treetops allowed for some light through, mostly fat beams from gaps in the canopies and lesser patches of sunshine. This gave the underlying foliage, roots, rough footpath, and tree trunks an exquisite look, as if a Pollack canvas for stippling sunlight.

"Not funny, Lucas!" Leila pushed me, and I dramatically staggered back onto the bridge.

The tableau of the trail behind her was suddenly replaced by just her. And I couldn't complain.

"Then why are you laughing?" I chuckled.

Leila exhaled, blowing a strand of hair out of her face, and placed both hands on her hips. She slumped to one side, and leered at me with her chin down a bit. That angle of her stare, under her brow, put me in a dilemma.

On one hand was the lovey-dovey route, complete with a sappy apology—even though we both knew I was just fooling around. And on the other was a more aggressive reaction, feeding the lust bubbling beneath my surface.

It was a win-win situation, really.

The only compromising factor was patience.

And god knew I'd been patient. But if there *was* a god or something of the sort, he or she would know, too, that I'd be patient for as long as it took. For what, exactly? I couldn't say, but I didn't really care, either. Every day was a blessing, and I wasn't down on my knees thanking some unseen deity for this life I lived.

No, I had solely Leila Pierce to thank, and the soaking red passion which bound us so inseparably.

"I'm sorry, baby," I sighed, taking the more patient option. I straightened myself out and approached her from the bridge. I stepped foot onto the softer earth, only to stop directly before her. "I didn't mean to startle you or anything. And you *know* I'd never…"

I stopped speaking, my lips continuing to move for a moment after, but carrying no sound.

Why?

Because she was suddenly trying to suppress something from boiling to the surface. Something too strong for her to stifle, something too buoyant and natural for even Leila Pierce to control.

That very thing began as a tiny smile which then effloresced into a grin spreading from one dimpled cheek to the other. The next stage was sound, a giggle creeping out of her mouth, seemingly carried by the poking tip of her tongue, between teeth. Simultaneously paired with an odd lisping noise produced by her lips.

All in the process of trying *not* to laugh.

And there I stood, the bringer of her stable insanity. A too beautiful thing.

"You can't hide from me, Leila," I jeered, moving in on her. Slowly at first, methodically. Hungrily.

I used my hands to tickle her, although the buttoned jacket made it less than effective. Regardless, she caved to the gesture and started laughing, all the while backpedaling away from me, and the bridge. Down the trail behind her.

She even pled for me to stop, her disposition nothing shy of lighthearted. Thus, I was unrelenting.

Finally I backed her into a tree beside the trail. It was a fat oak with rugged bark and a knot a few feet above us, giving it some personality. A perfect bystander to witness what was about to unfurl.

Better yet, there were no low branches.

A *clean* spot.

Though, not for long.

Finally my lips found their target, or at least one of many on a sinuous itinerary. I kissed the nook between her neck and shoulder and immediately all of our playful antics dissolved. What lurked beneath the surface, that bestial nature in each of us, shed its skin and leapt into action.

Leila assailed my hoodie with greedy hands, but it wasn't going anywhere. I wouldn't waste a second not pressed against her, so she diverted to target my jeans instead. I was quick to mirror her action, and within seconds we were both fettered by denim. The coolness of the air on my bare legs was actually refreshing.

Warmth was surging through me, anyway.

Adrenaline and blood pumping, engorging…

We kissed frenetically, not caring about hits or misses. Even when our lips or tongues went astray, it wasn't a loss. Our hands were not so different, either, groping and tugging at clothes, among other things, without fixating on one particular spot for longer than a couple of seconds.

Like two blind students covered in braille, learning to read in haste.

This aimlessness had its pros and cons. Before long, however, I vaulted it in search of something more established. The inescapable flesh.

My fingers curled between buttons and forced them apart. They were the clasping kind, so they didn't break, but the harshness of their detachment was still a soft echo. Leila gasped at the same time, a moist sound, and glanced down. My hands ascended the outside of her shirt, a black tee, until they found their targets.

Though arguably small, Leila's breasts were a favorite delicacy. Not just of my taste buds, but the hunger in my palms and fingers.

As I squeezed them outside of the shirt, grateful for her absence of a bra, I felt her eyes jerk up, and a lecherous stare barreled into me.

Her hands plummeted, frigid and soft to where I was just the opposite, and she seemed to relish these contrasting elements with her own thirst.

Even as I savored her escapist nipples through cotton, likely erect from the cold *and* titillation, my mouth salivated at the sight of her face. Every tic of arousal and excitement complemented her already gorgeous features.

My mouth zeroed in on hers to imbibe every billowing breath.

At last, my hands absconded from her perky breasts to hook the backs of her knees, and lift both legs. Her ankles locked behind me, Vans still on. I stepped closer, my own feet awfully close, and rerouted my hands. I gripped her partially exposed buttocks, cherishing the small pair of black panties she wore.

If anything was going to grate the bark behind her, it would be my knuckles and not her skin.

A due sacrifice.

I relished the sight of her face distort with wordless pleasure as I drove myself forward, and we each reveled in a mutual warmth, while the cold atmosphere cradled us.

As I thrusted, we shared panting breaths, and intermittently leaned in for a kiss. Or several. They were often so awry it almost made the exchange more heated, both literally and figuratively.

Before Leila's first series of moans, the only sound violating the wooded tranquility was the slapping of our skin, and the saturated union of our unashamed flesh.

As soon as she did begin moaning, it was an uproarious storm on a warpath, heralding rapture. It evoked from me sounds that I wouldn't expect myself to make, and together we foreshadowed our own climaxes through voice alone.

No words at first.

When they finally came, so did we.

Leila first, caving to the sensation as opposed to holding out as she often did. Her grip on me, in every fashion, lightened. Inside, inundated contractions made sure I would not last for long.

As her body trembled like quicksand, I felt myself be pulled into its depths of no return.

Cramps seized my thighs and the clashing of bark against my knuckles had to be close to drawing blood. In that moment, I couldn't care less.

Although spent, Leila was not checked out. She still savored my trip to that same destination.

She was just beginning to catch her breath, when I finally arrived.

I withdrew from her only to melt into her arms, emptying myself at the base of the tree, beneath her. The sodden warmth from her own climax now rubbed my lower stomach, my hoodie disheveled and crumpled around my waist.

I moved her hair to kiss her neck, her ear, and eventually our lips clashed, gently.

"Wow," she smiled.

"Good, or bad?" I asked, half-joking.

A man had to be sure. Stupid as he might be to even have to ask.

"What do you think, Lancelot?" She said rhetorically, a small simper on her face.

I chuckled. "Point made."

Her mouth dripped open, beckoning mine again. I kissed a potential response from it, savoring her bottom lip especially. It was a slow, molassic, quixotic gesture that I would never tire from.

Eventually, though, the creeping cold got the better of us, and we tacitly chose to stop. I let her down, and took careful steps back, hoisting up my boxers and jeans. Cautious of her own footing, she did the same, including the refastening of her jacket.

"So, we gonna finish this walk or not?" She asked, while I had my back turned. I had just finished fastening my jeans and straightening out my hoodie.

I turned on my heel to see her already continuing on-ward, down the trail, waving her arms at her sides and taking long strides. A runway model without a care in the world, a cat who would always land on her feet, no matter how elegant or inelegant her other steps were.

Careless and shameless in everything she did.

"Why the hell not?" I shrugged, and followed her, with a bounce in my own gait.

I caught up and snagged her by the waist, pulling her into me. We shared a giggle, and with her head turned, then a kiss.

Together, we proceeded to walk through the forest, although it felt as if the *forest* was walking through *us*.

IV

Ten minutes passed before we decided to turn around. There was no deep contemplation or conversation about why we ought to, it just seemed as if we had exhausted our stay. Lovely as the trail had been, a creeping urge to return to the cabin couldn't be denied.

Perhaps we just wanted to continue savoring our privacy, beyond the eyes of a spectating wilderness.

Besides, the forest probably wanted to rest and keep to itself, especially after we violated it with our act moments ago. It wanted to shed that memory, unless by an off-chance it actually enjoyed watching us through brush and bark.

"Yeah, let's head back," Leila suggested, spinning herself into my arms. I kissed her brow and looked around.

At second glance, I realized the trail had become duller. Not to insult nature, but the path itself had flattened out and presented nothing but a linear route, blandly overgrown and barren of personality. It wasn't offering, or leading to, any refreshing sights.

Perhaps we just weren't being patient enough.

"You sure?" I asked.

She had asked me a minute ago herself.

We clearly were both hesitant, but the itch was persistent enough. A sudden laziness had snuck into our bones; not to be confused with fatigue. We simply wished to retreat to the cabin and further into each other's arms.

"Let's just be sloths for the rest of the day," she suggested. "Besides, we have all week."

At first I had been a little tentative myself, curious enough to inch forward and see what was around the proverbial next corner. Except there were no actual corners, besides the one not far behind us, which led back to the bridge. Ahead was no more than a seemingly endless path, the shafts of sunlight lessening with every twenty feet or so.

"Yeah, I'd like that," I said, caving to her desires—and my own. "Maybe come back tomorrow, bring the camera, too."

"And one of my canvases," she added, her dark eyes lighting up.

"That'd be nice. Strip you down, body paint, let you streak through the woods like a nymph…"

She gasped and we shared a laugh.

"You devil," she bared her teeth.

"I know what you meant, but," I said, squeezing her close. "I couldn't resist."

"You never can. I have a way."

I surrendered to a grin before kissing her. It was all lips and jaws, no tongue. An interesting and compelling force of sorts.

When our faces parted, we were subdued by a layer of innocence, which was nice to retreat into. Like a safety net that was always there, a safe space to resign and be our silly selves, content with what life had turned out to be for us.

Ever so grateful for each other.

We wore our smiles as we turned away from the trail to head back toward the bridge.

Suddenly a deer bolted across our path, less than ten feet away. A brown blur with a white flare at its tail. The fawn darted back into the woods to our left, vaulting over a thicket of brush, barely shaking it, and vanishing into the forest.

Leila and I both exclaimed on impulse.

Our startled reactions quickly faded into chuckling, and we jostled one another.

"Fuck me, that came outta nowhere," I said, catching my breath.

"Yeah, the *nowhere* surrounding us!" Leila practically laughed. Only to add: "Scared the *shit* outta me!"

"Clearly," I mocked.

"Right, like you didn't damn near jump out of your socks, too."

"Be that as it may," I said sarcastically, with nothing to follow but a shrug.

She smirked.

"Whew, now I'm *really* hungry," I added.

She raised an eyebrow before giving me a shove, just hard enough to send me back a few paces. I passed right over the pair of deer tracks in the dirt under my shoes, briefly drawing my eyes.

There were only two, meaning the animal had literally flown across the trail, landing only briefly.

I looked up to see Leila marching toward me, a deliciously diabolical look in her eyes.

"Hey, now, don't go flipping *me* over the bridge."

"I won't, I won't," she said. "I *promise*."

I hardly believed her. A snake in the grass, this one. Given the right angle and momentum, she very well could launch me over that railing.

Debatably petite as Leila was, it would be criminal to underestimate her ferocity. Especially under the most jarring of circumstances. Plus, she had a mean sucker punch. I wouldn't know from first-hand experience, but the girl she got into a scuffle with last summer was testament.

Particularly, her wrecked face.

"My Leila," I muttered, backpedaling.

Finally she caught up to me, and I turned to "catch" her midstride. My arm wrapped around her waist and we kind of wrestled, standing, for the next several strides. Eventually, as we neared the bend in the trail ahead, we came to terms and our playful throes melted into an amicable embrace.

By the time we turned the corner, we were walking side by side, our faces a work of mirth.

That was short-lived.

Two crows were on the bridge, pecking at something on the wood. A third, larger crow, was perched on the railing above them, overlooking its avian friends. Its head turned to witness our arrival, cawing discordantly.

"Fucking crows," Leila said with a tinge of disgust. There was some history there. When she was thirteen, her cat Churchill got loose and was struck by a car. When she found it, crows were going to town, and wouldn't scatter despite her screams.

She had evolved past her trauma, but still detested crows.

I put a hand on her shoulder, which glided to her cheek.

"I got this," I said, beaming like a madman.

"Lucas, don't," she tried not to smile.

Before she could stop me, or attempt to, anyway, I turned away from her and charged the bridge. Moreover, the crows. With my arms raised and my face twisted in a strange expression. They didn't budge at first, so the closer I got the more I put into it. I began spewing a wide range of loud noises; like a boogeyman trying to impress his boss, I went all out.

Indubitably disturbing the forest even more, but I subconsciously hoped that I was doing it a favor by getting rid of these foul scavengers.

Just as I arrived at our side of the bridge, the two crows on the ground fluttered off, cawing in their wake. A few black feathers were shed in the process, drifting down to the dirty water below. My shoes skidded to a halt, and I found myself staring right at the third crow on the guardrail. It was unmoving, except for a tilting head. Those emotionless, beady black eyes bore into me. And then, without warning, it cawed shrilly. Pinpricks of chills doused me.

I sneered and swung at it.

"Fuck off!" I snapped at the same time.

The crow hoisted itself airborne, thick wings driving it up. A loud caw let out as it flew toward the treetops.

There, it vanished through the canopies and into a beautiful sky it didn't deserve.

"Having fun?" Leila's voice startled me from behind. I turned to face her, relieved at least to see a smile on her face.

"Yeah, actually, I was." I played it off. I had encountered murders of them before, and even far bigger, meaner ravens, but never had any disturbed me as much as that one crow did.

I couldn't put my finger on it.

Nor did I care to, especially with Leila by my side. I hooked an arm around her, and we started to cross the bridge.

"The fuck!?" Leila suddenly blurted, stopping in her tracks and gawking down.

I started to question her, puzzled, and then followed her gaze.

The crows had been pecking at a dead cardinal, its corpse sprawled out on the bridge in a vulgar manner. A dark crimson puddle had mixed with the dirt clinging to its feathers and feet, insinuating that the crows had transported it here. Worst of all, the cardinal's residual flesh was teeming with maggots.

Maggots, already?

It had hardly been twenty minutes since we left this area. Even if the crows had brought the cardinal here, its poor body and blood seemed fresher than the hours it took for maggots to form.

Despite Leila's disgust and aversion to crows, she found herself too bewildered to look away. She even knelt to inspect it more closely.

"Leave it alone, Leila, let's go," I sighed, shaking my head.

"It's dead, but for how long?" She said, pushing her hair over her ears. At least she kept her hands to herself. The repulsion and puzzlement in her voice was thick. "I don't get it, we were just—"

"I know, babe, and you got me," I said, but stopped pussyfooting. I stooped to pick her up, with a hand under her arm. "C'mon, let's head back to the cabin."

Finally she gave in and stepped over the macabre cardinal, walking with me. We crossed the bridge and trekked onward. She started to glance over her shoulder but I squeezed her hand in consolation and she proceeded at my side.

Ultimately we exited the forest and returned to the main trail, hugged by treelines and tallgrass on either side of us.

"That was…brutal," Leila said under her breath, clinging to me.

"Yeah," I sighed.

I was still a little shaken by it all but I could tell, already, that Leila was stepping out of it herself.

"But," I added, taking a deep breath. "Animals will be animals."

Leila smirked, her tongue clicking against her teeth.

"And we'd know," she said, nudging me.

A passage of laughter bridged any gap that had formed between us, and we jauntily came within view of the cabin. Eagerly, she leapt out in front of me, bounding up the hill and then the porch steps. She flung both doors open and shuffled inside.

She had not locked either of them when she left earlier. Out here, why bother?

I shut them behind me and stepped out of my shoes, next to where she had discarded hers. I then looked up and glimpsed her vanish into our room.

"Are you hungry?" I asked, half-sarcastically.

"Noooo!" She drawled lightheartedly.

I inched into the room, standing in the open doorway. The threshold was a space between the partition shared with the den, to my right, and the kitchen counter to my left, the rest of it behind me.

Suddenly Leila's stripped Drop Dead jacket landed on my head. I smirked and peeled it off, watching her step out of her jeans.

"Then whaddya wanna do?" I asked, tossing the jacket onto the bed.

"Watch a movie?" She asked, shrugging and smiling casually. "Your pick."

"Sure," I said. "I'll bear that weight."

She chuckled as I left the room.

Since we only brought five movies with us—all VHS for the sake of being compatible with the cabin's only TV—I wasn't faced with a difficult decision. Two were horror, one with a comedic theme, and another two were action-comedies. The fifth was strictly funny, beginning to end, so it was an easy choice for me.

Something to roll us back into our good mood.

Relaxed, but happy.

The usual catalyst to a great time.

I slipped the tape into the television's VCR player. The TV was a decent thirty-two-inch analog set, with a walnut trim on top of a wooden cabinet. I spent too long searching for the damn remote, by which time Leila strolled into the living room.

"Why, hello beautiful," I said, looking over my shoulder at her. She had stripped down to a white tanktop, no bra, and gray sweatpants that rode low on her hips. Her stance slumped to one side and waited for me, hands up under her chin.

"C'mon, Lucas," she pled.

"Just a sec, trying to get this POS started." I fumbled with the VCR and TV, abandoning hope of finding the remote at least for starters.

"Okay," she said in her mousy voice, and I heard her plump down onto the couch behind me.

I finally solved the VCR dilemma only to painfully step on the remote en route back to the couch. I cursed under my breath while Leila giggled from the couch. It sufficed to mitigate any iota of stress and I scooped it up to begin preparing the movie. I hit the FF button to skip through all the previews. Images of movies long past fled from us in the television, running into a hereafter of old movie stars and bad critics.

The flick we were about to watch was eight years old. Even so, it didn't feel like that long ago.

"Lemme go get changed, babe," I said, setting the remote down on the couch arm beside her. I then kissed her on the head before rerouting to the bedroom. "I'll be back in time for the movie!"

"You better," she said.

I disappeared from her line of sight, into our bedroom, and discarded my jeans. I swapped them for much more comfortable board shorts, while keeping my socks on. I removed my hoodie and layer of shirts in exchange for a plain black tee, then ambled back into the den.

I casually hurdled over the back of the couch, making it teeter only for a split-second, and plopped down beside Leila. She giggled and curled up next to me, as I slung an arm around her and looked at the TV.

I was just in time for the "feature presentation."

My free hand reached for the remote but it wasn't there.

"Am I sitting on the damn remote?" I asked, hopping up to get it. But it wasn't on the cushion, nor under it. And then I stopped to look down at Leila, who was struggling to stifle a grin. "Leila. Gimme the remote, babe. Movie's about to start."

I glanced over my shoulder. The tape was still being fast-forwarded. Next were flashes of "warning" and "the views expressed in the commentary" screens. Soon to follow would be production company logos, then the credits, dear God, we could miss the credits!

I heightened this mawkish reaction with a theatrically fake sad face.

"Give it up, Leila," I said, half-asking, and still pouting. I had to admit, Leila often deserved an Academy nod with her pretenses, but the best I'd get were the Razzies.

"Maybe I don't wanna."

"Give..." I slinked closer. "It..." I extended my hands. "Up!" I moved in to extract the remote, wherever it might be. Through a fit of cackling, tickling, and flailing limbs, I spotted it resting on the cushion under her crossed legs. I snagged it and backed up all of a sudden, almost tripping on the coffee table. Then I regained my balance and pressed play just in time for the credits to do their thing at the beginning of the movie.

Finally I took a deep breath and collapsed onto the cushion next to Leila.

We hugged each other and locked our legs together, though I wished she wasn't wearing sweats. At any rate, we were tremendously comfortable and our shenanigans had simply wound us up to wind us down.

Despite how easily distracted by each other as we could be, especially the sight of her beheld by me, we managed to watch the movie with focused delight.

Gradually, time rested its pall over us. Our exhaustion brought our train home, but we were too cozy to exit the car. We fought off the urge to drift asleep, and continued watching the movie with heavy eyes and fleeting laughter. The potency of the latter grew increasingly weaker.

Still, we ran on the fumes of mirth and stayed awake. Just enough, at least, to last us to the end of the movie. Assuming we would make it.

As we watched, my mind wandered a little.

Sometimes I wondered how amazing it would be if the characters of a movie were actually living their own lives, like we did on a normal basis, only theirs were far more entertaining. And every now and then they would turn to face a camera looming at them, realizing they were being watched.

But in this peculiar reality, *we* were the ones being watched.

And so they would pretend we weren't there. They

proceeded to do their thing, solely to impress us. Although, more often than not, it was as if *they* were the ones entertained by *our* dullness. Our lack of willpower to turn away, our docility to just sit there for two hours watching them live their lives.

Of course, sometimes I wondered too much.

By the time the movie ended, all the laughter had left my stomach feeling a bit jumbled. So I peeled myself off the couch, and visited the kitchen. I wasn't sure if it was hunger or fatigue, but I chose to entertain the prior.

I snagged an apple from a drawer in the fridge, its cool smoothness, and even heft, already an appetizing sensation in my hand.

I bit into it, crisp as ever, and relished the cold juices flooding my mouth. I almost moaned from the taste, and knew that would've made Leila giggle if she was within earshot.

The sticky rivulets from the apple ran down its red skin and around my fingers. People really didn't realize how messy eating a single apple, by hand, could be.

I reclined against the counter and suddenly noticed that we hadn't turned on many of the lights when we got back from our walk earlier. It was early afternoon at the time, and beautifully sunny, so with curtains parted from most of the windows, there stood no purpose to.

I was close to finishing the apple and only then looked up to ask if Leila wanted a bite. She hadn't made a peep since I got up, so I presumed she had drifted off.

To my surprise, she wasn't on the couch.

I must not have noticed her get up, I was so intent on

devouring this damn apple.

I heard her shuffling in the bedroom and decided to pay an overdue visit. Unashamedly, I hoped she was getting changed.

The door hung ajar.

We rarely practiced such privacy, especially under the circumstances. This vacation of sorts was our way of shedding all of that.

Tentatively, I put a hand to the door.

"Babe? Can I come in?"

"Yeah, sure," she said lackadaisically.

I relaxed and entered. She was sitting on the other side of the bed, facing the window. It was open, but fortunately not as cold as earlier. I hardly felt it, even in my board shorts and shirt.

The near-finished apple had stopped seeping in my hand. I stood at the foot of the bed, and at least relished that Leila was completely naked, her *SOAKING RED* tattoo naturally catching my eye. Her short black hair was parted at the neck, strands flowing over either shoulder, barely the length to do so. Her barcode tattoo was partially visible.

"Ain't you cold, babe?" I asked.

Leila giggled and stood up to turn around.

I dropped the apple. It hit the floorboards but I barely even heard it. As if it had fallen a mile away. Leila's lower jaw was missing, in its place a half-eaten cardinal, squirming and squawking, somehow assimilated to her skull. Blood and maggots spilled from her mouth, and the bird's. Her head tilted to the side, until her neck cracked sickeningly at an unnatural angle.

My expression warped with disgust and terror, but alas my eyes locked with hers.

No, not hers.

They were small and black, lightless. Beady, like a crow's. Her nose was missing, too, but not as if it never existed. In its place were exposed nasal cavities, flaring and leaking blood that ran black.

The rest of her body was pristine.

"I'm not cold," she replied, somehow able to speak normally. "I'm so very fucking hot."

Chills razed my spine.

Breath struggled to find its exit from my lungs, as my body froze in horror. Shock seized my every bone and muscle.

Somehow, through her grisly face, she grinned, only to reach out for me. At the same time, she regurgitated the cardinal, projectile vomiting it at me. I screamed so hard and fast my throat hurt, while the sound rang in my ears and as if caused by my reaction, the window behind her slammed shut. Glass shattered, spraying her backside. She screamed, too, but it quickly turned into a weeping wail before she suddenly collapsed, all the terrible things about her evaporating like condensation, slowly drifting to the floor.

Among them, a pale feather spattered with ink and blood.

I sunk to my knees and caught her falling body, but it never reached my arms.

Sharp, raspy breaths clogged my throat as I woke, sprawled out on the couch. The TV screen was black, the VCR making a dull running sound, the tape nearing its end. Leila was there with me, her head resting on my chest.

I caught my breath and to my relief, as well as surprise, she had somehow not been stirred awake by me.

Then again, she *was* a notoriously heavy sleeper. Still, on an impulse, I checked her vitals. Wrists read fine. I looked her over, and she was as she always was, absolutely gorgeous.

Just tired.

I reclined and stretched out my legs, heart steadying, both in my chest and temples.

A deep, but calm, breath escaped me.

What in the fuck was *that*?

Gingerly, I got up from the couch. I made sure the sleeping Leila was comfortable. She appeared a tad cold, scrunched up next to where I had been. With no blankets set out yet, I quietly moved into the bedroom. The first thing I laid my eyes upon was the shut window opposite the bed.

I tried to comfort myself with reassurances, but couldn't shake a disturbed feeling. My stomach ached and the images from the nightmare wouldn't leave my mind. I had never had such a dream before.

Fucking hell.

Focusing on Leila helped alleviate me, at least. So I turned to the bed, to pull an excess blanket off and take it back into the den with me.

My foot kicked something across the floor.

I looked down and saw an apple core rolling across the floorboards. It stopped against the far wall, near my dresser.

My stomach lurched and a sea of chills enrobed me. I scuffled toward it, picked it up with haste and anger, but was at least relieved there were no bugs. Or maggots.

Urgently, I returned to the kitchen and dumped it into the trash bin. I tasted bile and spun on my heel to rush toward the bathroom, but not the one attached to the bedroom. This one was smaller, and had a door. Which I immediately shut, without slamming. Subconsciously I hoped all of this movement hadn't stirred Leila.

That thought disintegrated as I knelt in front of the toilet and vomited into the water. I gave in, as opposed to fighting it. In hopes that the purgation was of more than just the sick feeling, but the horrid images, too.

Once I was done, I used a strip of toilet paper to wipe my mouth, then dropped it into the bowl, and hit the flush handle. Disoriented, albeit less than before, I watched my insides twirl around in the disgusting water until it all vanished into the unseen abysses below.

I knew that I didn't want to see it all, anyway. A cesspool of the foulest things imaginable, and the way my mind was lately, probably so much more.

And all the better I not look too deep.

"Lucas?" I heard her voice from the other side of the door, but by the sound of it a little farther than that. A few paces into the den, probably still on the couch.

"Yeah?" I said, trying to sound normal.

I felt I had managed to pass it off. I stood up, quietly closing the toilet lid and making sure my mouth was clean. It was the only time I would ever refuse a kiss from her.

"Where are you?" She asked.

"Bathroom," I replied, and turned on the sink. It was wall-mounted and without a mirror above it, unlike the pedestal one in our room. I went to run the warm water, and the pipes in the walls groaned. I mumbled "okay, okay" and turned the cold knob, holding my hands under the faucet. The crisp water made my hands tremble even more, working against my own efforts to stabilize myself.

They shook less as I unboxed the soap bar on the side of the faucet, taking deep breaths. After washing my hands quickly, trying to forget about the apple, I turned the sink off and looked around. I shook my head and dried my hands on my shorts. We hadn't even put out any towels in here just yet. The TP and soap were provided. It was basically a closet with a toilet and sink. We didn't intend on using it much, but there still definitely needed to be a handtowel.

I turned toward the door and heard the floorboards creak on the other side.

"You alright?" Leila asked, sounding worried.

"Yeah, just had to take a piss," I said, hating to lie. I threw on a fake smile and opened the door to face her. As casual and natural as she looked, the simple sight was enough to turn my façade into truth. The smile and contentment, anyway. The lie, I only stretched out. "I mean, imagine…all the sex this morning, the glass of milk, sex in the woods, hours pass…felt like my bladder was gonna burst."

Leila laughed briefly. In that interim, I suddenly wished I had in fact gone pee. Dammit.

"Right," she nodded. "I was just wondering, 'cause I thought I heard something in the bathroom."

Probably vomit spattering toilet water.

"Yeah, that was my bladder reaching its limit. I feel *so* much better."

I laughed it off and dodged a kiss from her, a sly move I had mastered over the years, given moments like these. Well, far less disturbing, of course. She ultimately kissed my cheek and I nuzzled her neck, imbibing her scent like a refreshing, therapeutic aroma.

We hugged and teetered on opposing feet.

I reached down and casually fondled her butt, outside of the sweatpants. I felt her lips spread across her face, forming a smile, against my own.

"Well, are you hungry at all?" She asked.

"Nah, my stomach feels a bit upturned. Maybe in an hour or two." I squeezed in a morsel of honesty, at least. "How are *you* doing?"

"Good, actually. Still kinda tired, though. I'm gonna go take a nap in the bed, proper like. My neck is kinda cramped from passing out on the sofa. Do you know how long we were asleep?"

I shrugged. "Twenty minutes, maybe. Just at the end of the movie."

"Huh. Well, still a good flick. Funny as shit."

We shared another chuckle, genuine from my end, too, and then she disengaged to head for the bedroom.

"I might actually join you in a bit," I said after her. "Just gonna get a drink of water then see how I feel."

"Okay, baby," she said, pausing by the doorway leading into our room. "Have some water, just not too much. I like my sheets the way they are."

This time, my laugh was fake.

I proceeded into the kitchen as she entered the bedroom, and most of me envied her obliviousness, as well as her blasé surrender to lassitude.

I snagged a water bottle from the fridge, and uncapped it. My eyes drifted up to have a glance into the bedroom. Thanks to the floorplan and open doorway, from the kitchen I could see Leila sitting at the foot of the bed. She pulled off her sweatpants, exposing those milky legs, and then turned, butt out, before crawling onto the bed.

Me oh my.

I might just be ready to join her sooner rather than later.

Bottoms up, Aquafina.

V

After conquering two bottles of water, I for sure had to urinate. I used the same bathroom as before, hoping to not wake Leila, who made non-snoring sleepy sounds from the bedroom. Never short of adorable. Unfortunately, after my use of the bathroom, I still felt a bit restless. The lethargic sensation in my body, and even in corners of my mind, was stubbornly persistent.

Not to mention the nightmare, unlike anything I had ever experienced before, of that nature.

It certainly made me less avid to fall asleep again, although beside Leila, in "our bed," was rationally tempting.

Still, I didn't want to risk disrupting her serenity of sleep with my restlessness.

To better clear my head, I took a seat on the couch and stared at one of the windows behind the television set. The curtains were parted and through the dirty panes I could see the clear afternoon sky. It was still relatively sunny, but time was slipping closer and closer toward dusk. It was minutes to four o'clock last I checked.

Outside the window and beyond the cabin swayed treetops in the wind.

Apparently a strong enough breeze to persuade even

those towering oaks to bend, and shudder their lush canopies. It was as if some omnipotent deity or enormous cloaked giant was watching the cabin, breathing steadily, his exhalations affecting the trees.

If this was in fact the case, I did wonder what his intentions were. Because as of late, I had my doubts. It was quite unfortunate considering how great the last few days had been, including the ones we spent preparing and even hitching our way up here. What was normally a stressful preamble to our actual vacation had been a fun experience.

And this morning alone, nothing to complain about.

I had to admit, one of the best I had ever spent with Leila.

I tried to relax more. These notions certainly helped. I excavated that optimism which had tunneled its way beneath my feet earlier. It was cowering from the nightmare, from the apple core, and it probably began its initial descent when we came across the cardinal on the bridge.

At last, with the optimism resurfacing and gasping for a fresh breath, I recovered my key to success. Motivation. The objective that Leila and I had set our sights on, upon vacationing here: to have a damn good time. To escape, not just from the world, but into each other.

So far, it seemed we had.

With the exception of the last hour or two, I knew *I* had, and from the looks of it, Leila was faultlessly enjoying herself, too.

The most important thing of all to me.

I just had to catch up.

Sitting there on the couch, I felt my body grow more

tired by each passing second. Time plodded by in heavy boots, dripping tar, little anvils like anchors glued to their soles, clogging the treads and dragging in the mud. It didn't take long for my eyelids to capitulate and droop. My gaze drifted from the window to the black TV screen to the blank wooden wall of the cabin to the closed front door and, finally, to nothing at all.

Don't you hate it when you sleep for hours on end, or even a mere thirty minutes, and then wake up with no recollection of dreams? Just a thoughtless void spitting you out, chewed up and often feeling more tired than you were when you first crashed?

It wasn't an uncommon dilemma, I knew that much.

Which presently made me a statistic.

I remembered dozing off, feeling the weight of fatigue and physical helplessness overpower me. I remembered thinking about Leila, the nightmare I had experienced, the apple core, the strong wind outside, the nightmare—

My eyelids went from faintly open to agape, and I felt a burst of energy surge through me. I sprang from the sofa and, ignoring the cramps holding my limbs hostage, scrambled toward the bedroom.

I entered and came to a stop before making too much more noise. To my relief, Leila was snuggled up in bed, clutching a pillow, fast asleep.

I took a few deep breaths, my heart redlining at first. As it decelerated, I planted my back against the doorjamb, and overlooked the bed. The white comforter was tossed aside, but underlying sheets were pulled up to Leila's neck. She was facing the other wall, the outline of her half-naked form against the sheets a joy to perceive.

And a fleeting thought of relief.

In its wake came a notion of just the opposite. A subconscious reminder that I could, quite possibly, be having a nightmare right now. I wouldn't know until something abysmal happened, right?

Not the kind of confirmation I wanted.

"Fuck me," I muttered under my breath.

My head tilted back and knocked the doorjamb. I caught my breath, steadied my pulse, and closed my eyes. I opened my mental gateway to pleasant memories of Leila and me, from the previous day to the previous year, and everything wonderful in between. From the smallest smiles to the biggest orgasms. The memories flooded my mind like a river with no dam, profuse with rainbow trout and magical fish that had yet been named.

I could hardly even feel the faint smile creep onto my face as I bathed myself in these memories.

Perhaps I wasn't even smiling, I just imagined that I was.

Afterall, with memories like those, how couldn't I? And knowing Leila was in my life in any capacity, had a stupendous healing power of its own.

Then a familiar blackness overcame me, and I had no recollection of ever actually hitting the floor.

"Lucas…Lucas!" Her voice echoed in my skull before I realized it was hovering over me.

"Leila?" I said groggily.

"Lucas, wake up!"

"I'm so tired, though…what's wrong?" My brow furrowed. My vision was still dark. Was I too exhausted, too weak to open my eyes?

"Please, baby, wake up."

Something wet touched my lips. It actually tasted kind of good, familiar, with a scent I recognized as well. I whimsically kissed back. Something slipped into my mouth. A tongue?

Suddenly it withdrew.

My eyelids finally fluttered open.

"Yeah, of course *that* wakes you up," Leila said, her frustration discernible through a brief chuckle.

I realized she was kneeling in front of me, between my extended legs, wearing black jeans and a white Bebe T-shirt. Not to mention a sullen expression.

"Wha…" I smacked my lips, trying to seize my voice despite cottonmouth. "What's wrong, Leila?"

"First of all, why are you sleeping against the couch?"

My brow furrowed. "What? Where?"

I thought I passed out in the doorway?

I pivoted my head, feeling aches jolt through my neck. Turned out I was sitting on the floor with my back and head flat against the left side of the couch, facing a windowless wall. If I was on the other side of the sofa, I'd be facing the foyer and kitchen.

"Lucas," Leila asked, slowly and solemnly. "Are you okay?"

"Yeah, I mean…" I cleared my throat and looked up at her. "Yes, babe, I am. Just…tired as hell."

"And hungry, too, huh?"

"What?" I raised an eyebrow.

"When I found you a minute ago, you had three apple cores in your lap. I threw them away. Kinda gross, baby."

My mind raced, heart trying to escape my chest. I couldn't recall even a blur of visiting the kitchen, let alone retrieving three apples and devouring them. That would've taken time, too…

It *would* explain my cottonmouth, though.

Not that it could be dismissed so easily. Even that explanation would need an explanation. Nothing made sense.

"To be honest," she sighed. "You don't look so hot. No offense."

"None taken. I don't feel hot. Or cold, for that matter. I just feel wrought."

Leila's brow furrowed. Part in concern, and part in confusion.

"I dunno, I dunno," I said, shaking my head and feeling my temples jackhammer. "What I *do* know is that I have a killer headache, I remember passing out on the couch after drinking some water, then again in the bedroom doorway, now this. And I—"

She started waving her hands.

"Wait, wait, wait. You passed out in our bedroom? And *before* that, the couch?"

"Yeah. Really tired. I got up…I got up from the couch, I think I'd only slept for like thirty minutes, then went over to the room and saw you sleeping there. I didn't wanna wake you but I *was* gonna get in bed with you. Then I…"

Not a liar, lying.

"I don't know, I just felt so exhausted, I guess I blacked out."

Four weeks ago we had gone literally an entire day doing nothing but fucking at home, taking walks, and fucking in parks, and I was buoyant until two the next morning.

Everything that had transpired today was nothing in comparison. It was the nightmare, and the hallucinations, that were really wearing me down.

I just didn't want to divulge that to her, I didn't want to tarnish her with the unsettling truth.

Leila began shaking her head, very slowly. Pensively. Her eyes dropped and she briefly kneaded her temples before taking one of my hands in her own.

She was deeply worried about me, but I could suddenly tell there was something else wrong. Something she wasn't telling me.

Which only made me feel worse about my own secret, especially if I could get her to excavate hers. And I needed to.

"What's wrong, babe?" I asked, leaning forward and gently squeezing her hands with mine, lifting another to touch her cheek. Meanwhile, my cramps and aches started to slowly dissipate. My puzzled concern for her was a greater pain. "Leila, look at me. My love. Something else—what is it?"

Leila swallowed.

"I had a nightmare," she said, her eyes lifting to me. My stomach knotted at that last word. I tried not to show it, while she spoke. "Christ, it was…it was *bad*, Lucas. I thought I was actually awake, but I wasn't. Of course, *I* didn't know this, at the time. But I got out of bed and there was…"

Apparently, she had repressed the memory of this nightmare and was likely distracted from it by finding me with the apples. Like Adam sympathy-eating for Eve. But now, it was all surfacing, and at the same time, sinking its talons into her.

Her gaze diverted from me as she recalled every detail, and rambled them out. Simultaneously, tears began to well up in her eyes.

My skin crawled as I listened and watched, my gut hurting even more.

"There was a deer, Lucas. In our bed. Its entire body, a little fawn. B-Blood, everywhere. The sheets were *drenched*. Y-You weren't there, just this deer. I woke up screaming and I, I thought it was me but it was the deer. It was *screaming*. I jumped out of bed and cried out your name, running, trying to find you. I ran s-*straight* out the fucking door…"

Tears streaked her cheeks, voice trembling.

"And there you were," she said, with a disturbed chuckle that immediately warped her face into a terrible frown. "At the base of the porch steps, butt-naked, standing over Gabe, chopping him up with a f-fucking *axe*. You turned around and smiled at me, asking that I join you. Asking…Asking me to join you."

Leila broke down in tears and crumpled against me. I threw my arms around her like a fire blanket. Although I wasn't sure just how well I could protect her, given my own hallucinations. I would nonetheless try my damnedest, and there was nothing I could think of that might stop me from trying.

This caliber of nightmares, however, was new to me. And Leila, I would assume. We didn't have secrets between us.

Except for the one I was currently keeping under wraps. *My* nightmares. Now, doing so served no purpose.

Gabe, she had mentioned him.

Gabriel Weismann was Leila's boyfriend before me. A year and a half before we met, their relationship—in every possible way—ended.

They only dated a few months. At the end of which, when she tried to break it off due to his violent tendencies, he reported to her AA sponsor that she had violated her sobriety. Days later he assaulted her, his intentions rape. She wound up in the hospital, but his fate was worse. She killed him in self-defense with a snub-nosed revolver, which she had bought for a couple hundred during the time he was stalking her.

That was Gabe's story.

When I said earlier that she and I had our troubles, I wasn't exaggerating. The demons of our pasts were not unbeknownst to each other, and upon falling in love we forgave ourselves, one another, and had long since buried them.

Leila had her alcoholism, and then that Gabe debacle she managed to survive. Both mortally and lawfully.

I, on the other hand, had my heroin. The day I met Leila I'd been sober for ten months and three weeks. Believe it or not I was struggling with notions of relapse, too. She changed all of that. An unprecedented high, being in love with her. Finally, a healthy addiction. One that revitalized me, from beginning to end, instead of destroying me from within.

Unfortunately, I had my own dark secrets when we met. She was an angel helping me through them.

During the expanse of my addiction, I had taken two lives, and I wore full responsibility for them. Vehicular manslaughter, DUI, seven years ago. Hit-and-run, with friends in the car. *Friends*, right; more like connections, minus emotional loyalty.

We were never caught. Legally, anyway. For years to come, I served a prison in my own mind.

At that time, though, I was the only one among us crying. I had been driving, besides. I was so young, and suddenly felt younger, having taken a life out of stupidity and negligence. A failed suicide attempt months later resulted in even heavier heroin abuse.

Before submitting to a sobriety program, the group I ran with—the fucking parasites they were, we all were for that matter—tried to execute a coup on our dealers. Simply because they had refused to sell to us anymore; a just call, looking back on it. Not to say that dealers of that disease were ever sound in judgement to begin with. At any rate, we were never caught for anything we did that night.

Two of us killed two of theirs. There had been three. I killed the third with a .38 Special.

Leila was not alone, as both of our pasts were tainted, mine arguably worse. We had long since mustered the strength and love to move beyond them, though, finding a panacea to our demons in the form of our bond.

Of course, I couldn't say that either of us were absolved of regret. Regret was something I still didn't fully understand, a sickness in and of itself.

What we believed was the key to the death of regret was fixating on, and practicing, love over hate. Toward others, and toward the self.

As for repentance, perhaps it wasn't meant to be a black-and-white thing. Perhaps it came later in life, or even after it, in some incomprehensible fashion not meant for the mortal mind.

Through exercising love over hate, however, one could truly find happiness, or at least their version of it. Leila and I had both come to genuinely believe this.

Afterall, we were.

Happy.

So what in the hell was *this*?

"Leila, Leila," I said, rubbing her shoulders as her sobs faded. Tears had dappled her white T-shirt. Her black denim-clad legs were sprawled between mine. I was still in my own shirt and shorts. In this moment of weakness, however, I knew I needed to bare myself to her, right down to the bone.

As much as I feared it might just worsen her emotions, and break us down, rung by rung.

I had to see the strength in truth, and making sure she didn't feel so alone in her distress.

And then her lips happened.

They collided with mine, and her lamentations metamorphosed into something higher. Grander. An expression of our love, not our lust. Not at first anyway. It was this desperate attempt to salvage her humanity by melting into me, and goddammit if I didn't do the same. She was, afterall, my tourniquet. And I hers.

I should've used my words.

But I was a weak man to her ways of the flesh, of the heart, and how her fervent soul swam in tandem with mine.

In that extended, wet, warm breath, I had just about forgotten the nightmares which demanded us to believe in them. I shoved those things aside, as if to say "fuck you, *this* is real, *our love* is real, not the fear."

Fuck fear.

We fell into each other's embrace, toppling and splaying across the floorboards. Unyielding and as far from comfortable as one could imagine, but somehow smooth, not coarse. No splinters. And our bodies sufficed as both cushions and blankets.

Our hands fumbled, fondled, and grabbed aimlessly. Our mouths did the same. Eyes shut, trusting in each other's darkness. Marrying ours into one shared subconscious.

Before I could even begin to count the seconds that had passed, or dare I say minutes, I was on my back and Leila above me like some kind of wingless angel still capable of flight. She had tugged her jeans down past her hips, and the buttonless fly of my shorts was an effortless gateway for my excitation.

We joined and my fingers sunk into the flesh of her hips. Her thighs smacked mine, and she moved with both a grace and a bluntness I couldn't match with words.

Nor could our mouths.

Breathy moans of speechless surrender.

Curtained by her dangling hair, her brown eyes somehow retained an iota of light. They twinkled as our stares locked, and I wasn't sure if it was a wetness from her tears or something more astral. Perhaps both. An amalgamation of human and cosmic features.

Finding a home in this very moment.

So very tragically beautiful.

Our movements became just as fierce as they were an expression of dedition. It was a stupefying, intoxicating limbo between lovemaking and feral sex.

It was literally an escape from reality.

And never before had our reality warranted such an aggressive escape.

Until now.

Like any escape, though, it wasn't endless. Culmination tempted my body to capitulate for a final blast of pleasure. Sensing that Leila hadn't arrived at that point just yet, I exercised both patience and conviction, slowing down.

I adjusted my body against the floor and my hands rose to her waist. My thumbs dug for purchase and I lifted her off of me. Mildly cool air, at least compared to her insides, chilled my loins. I saw her gnaw a bottom lip before looking down, between our bodies, and exhaling a staggered moan.

Methodically, I let her back down, reentering her fuchsia lair and letting it close around me.

She whimpered delectably and I sat up to rob her breath for a place in my throat. Our kiss burgeoned into something rabid and uninhibited, a libidinous entity disembodied between us, but trapped for our own use.

We were relentless in our ensuing motions.

Pursuing the same cause, I miraculously helped Leila achieve her sliver before mine.

I gave an abrupt thrust as our mouths disengaged, and felt her body shudder on top of mine. The F-word sundered from her lips like a wave breaking against a mighty galleon.

Seconds later, as her tepid currents coursed over me, I witnessed a faint smile make its way onto her face. I couldn't help but mimic it in all genuineness.

Yet within my chasms of skepticism, given our recent hallucinations, I pondered its reality.

Then again, if *it* wasn't real, then *none* of this was. And I couldn't accept that. Her littlest smile was my biggest rapture, and I embraced it wholeheartedly.

I gave in, via a series of rattling thrusts. Leila gasped and rode it out, or at least she believed she was. But that very thing buried inside me wasn't quite ready for release. It wouldn't be jettisoned so soon.

With a burst of energy, I sprang to my feet, albeit not without a brevity of inelegance. I staggered for a second, the side of the couch bracing me. I righted my stance and, with both hands gripping Leila's butt, her right calf over her left shin behind me, I carried her across the den. Our skin bumped, our laps still sharing the same intimacy.

She giggled into my ear, some of her hair sticking to my face.

As I entered our bedroom, I recognized it as nothing less than our temple. I exterminated all images of dead deer and rotting cardinals from my mind as I set Leila down on the sheets. She looked so at home there, her pale form upon a sea of white fabric.

Spectacular as it was to witness, I was emptied of patience.

I fell into position, her head resting on a pillow, eyes lifted to me. Dimming sunlight from outside illuminated the room with a cool shade.

Only at first, I thrusted intermittently.

I stared down at her, and without kissing those lips I could taste the tears. The sweat, the pain, the pleasure. The passion.

Everything that was *Leila*.

And then I exploded.

I realized I had been holding my breath. I let it out, and my heartbeat found its footing. I could hear blood rushing through the veins in my head, like a million microscopic horses galloping at once. I looked down and saw my work, profuse and alabaster on Leila's disheveled shirt.

Gradually, everything slowed to the reasonable pace that was normal life.

I rolled off to the side, while she dispensed of her shirt, and then relaxed beside me. The both of us on our backs, eyes up at the ceiling, arms touching. Several indeterminable seconds passed, lost in that moment.

"I love you," I said quietly, my gaze still up.

I felt the mattress shift slightly to accompany new movement, and looked over to see that Leila had scooted considerably closer. Her exposed breasts grazed my clothed chest.

"Lucas," she said, staring into my half-open eyes. She began to say something else, the three words I had just said, but I interrupted her. I couldn't help it.

"I love you, Leila," I repeated, my head turning to reciprocate her gaze.

Her eyes welled up. Her lips twitched, starting to form a smile, but it devolved into a weak frown.

"I know you do," she said, her voice delicate. "And I love you, too. You *know* I do."

"I couldn't bring myself to believe in any other thing as strong as I do that, Leila." I lifted a hand and the knuckles of my fingers brushed her cheek. "I always have. I've never doubted your love, as much as I felt unworthy of it early on, and I never will second-guess it. No matter what happens, I'll always love you beyond the four-letter word we associate it with."

Speechless, Leila leaned in to kiss me softly on the lips. A gesture and a flavor subtle and simultaneously momentous. Ones I would never grow weary of.

"I don't know what's going on, Lucas, but it doesn't matter. It's just a strange phase. We're strong, you and I. And together…we're fucking invincible."

My eyes welled up, too.

Fuck.

Instead of cowering from it, I wore my blurred vision with an odd sense of pride, and cupped her cheek. I guided her face to mine, but she also leaned in on her own volition. We exchanged little kisses.

Our arms followed, bodies pressing together, arms overlapping. We kicked off our bottoms and then I discarded my shirt, so that our nakedness could be one.

I heard Leila whisper "I love you" once again in my ear. And shortly thereafter, a slumber I was anticipating but no longer fearing crept over me.

I could only trust that Leila would follow suit; if anything, she'd fall asleep sooner than me.

As my mind and body were engulfed in that final step of weariness, I tried to envision my own dream. As a means of warding off bad thoughts, but also as a reflex from what we just experienced.

Eyes shut and Leila in my arms, our bodies warmly entangled, I pictured the two of us being happy. As we were, but outside. Hands together, walking and laughing. Autumn leaves skittering across the pavement around our feet.

Then I changed course.

I reconstructed it.

I imagined Leila as a child, with her mother. A woman I never had the chance to meet. I nonetheless arranged them in my dream, with benevolent omnipotence. They were playful, getting along famously. According to Leila, the childhood she never had. But in my dreams, she was so fortunate.

Somewhere along the road, I would imagine the two of us further in the future. Older but healthy. Slow and steady, our love unsullied by time. I smiled at the notion. I smiled and I tried to sleep the way we were meant to sleep.

And whatever might happen from there would not be my doing.

VI

Our bedside alarm clock was not really used for waking us up, not out here. Or even back home, unless we had an appointment or work. At the cabin, the clocks were provided and run-of-the-mill. There were a few analog sets on the wall here and there, but on our nightstand was a trapezoidal digital clock with a snooze button on top and an off switch on the side. The readout displayed ruby numbers not too harsh on waking eyes.

I was grateful for this as I groggily pulled myself out of my slumber. I stretched and yawned quietly, my vision adjusting.

According to the faithful clock, it was ten past eight, which explained the nightfall outside the window I was facing, and thus the general darkness of the room. Only moonlight filtering into the cabin, and a lamp on in the den, its yellowish glow oozing through the doorway, illuminated the room.

I was no mathematician, but I deduced we had slept for nearly four hours. Overdue, I'd say. Especially given the peacefulness that it was.

To my delight, not disappointment, Leila was still asleep. Her head was turned toward me, right side of her face mushed into the pillow she cuddled. Her hair a pretty dark mess around her pale face and shoulders, peeking above sheets.

I smiled to myself, and then another yawn hit me. I stretched again for the hell of it, only to slowly swing my legs out from under the sheets and quietly get to my feet. Tiptoeing, I gathered a pair of boxers and then slipped on my jeans. I pulled a T-shirt over my head en route to the den, nearly bumping into the door while the fabric shielded my eyes.

Dumbass.

I shook my head, pulled the shirt down, and quietly exited the room. I closed the door without shutting it, a mere inch or two between the lock and jamb. If I shut it all the way, even slowly, half this damn place would creak as if it was going to implode.

Stealth had been never a great forte of mine, but under the circumstances I'd make an exception.

One thing I didn't like was leaving the curtains open when it was past dark. In the city it made complete sense, but out here the argument wasn't the same. Especially if we didn't have our lights on. And even if we did, who or what were possibly spying on us?

Smokey the Fucking Bear?

I doubted we were interesting enough.

If anything, I'd be more compelled to "stargaze" except deep into the woods, between trees, and let my eyes toy with the shadows.

Perhaps not tonight, all things considered.

On my way to the windows around the den, to pull the curtains shut, I turned on the kitchen light and the ceiling fixture by the foyer. Afterall, I was feeling a little livelier now that I was well-rested, and everything I had shared with Leila, and exchanged, hours ago. It wasn't that I was just physically rejuvenated, but spiritually, too.

Which went so much further.

I couldn't have been more grateful that we slept for so long, undisturbed. What had seemed like just twenty minutes ago, I was thinking wonderful thoughts. And now there was a bounce in my step, despite it being eight at night, the rural moon glazing our cabin in its silvery glow.

Oh, how time passed.

As eager as I was to embrace and kiss Leila once she was up, and figure out how to spend our night, I would let her sleep indefinitely. She could wake naturally, just as I had.

After shutting the curtains to the window between the kitchen and front door, I crossed the den. Toward the window behind the TV, but before closing the curtains I took a longer moment to savor the placid sight of nightfall outside.

The brightness of the stars in the unpolluted, cloudless, blue-black sky were specks compared to the full moon suspended high. We had planned this trip accordingly, knowing how great it was to be out in the country when the moon was at its brightest. The weather forecast lined up and we were grateful these last two nights.

Whenever Leila got up, I knew she would love this view.

The moon was like a cyclops' upturned eyeball, his vivid iris currently hidden, and belonging to the sun. The night had subjected itself to the galactically colossal beast, for it was his time to nap.

And give those treetops a rest, too.

Many earthbound creatures were known to be nocturnal, though. Even sharks were among them, despite being submerged in water. Fortunately our cabin wasn't floating in the middle of the ocean.

Bats were also infamously active at night, and often felines as well.

I let my mind mull over this tangent while I closed the curtains and moved to the last window.

I strolled past the left side of the couch, where I had passed out earlier—fat question mark there—and toward the opposing wall. I walked a few feet down the length of it, where it extended into a narrow hall toward the backdoor. The wall to the left was a thick wooden partition behind our bed's headboard. Its density was sufficient for me to not worry about holding my breath or being unnecessarily quiet, for fear of waking Leila.

Nonetheless, I did glance at it and smile to myself, as if seeing through the wall and headboard to caress a peacefully sleeping Leila with my eyes alone.

Farther down the hall, in an alcove near the backdoor, were the washing machine, dryer, and water heater. The A/C unit was integrated into the back of the cabin, within a safe distance from the crank-shower.

I turned to the window on the wall opposite the one behind our headboard. To my far left, at the end of the narrow hall, was the backdoor, its own glass panes veiled by a cluster of beige curtains. I glimpsed the deadbolt's position, and that it was locked. Neither relieved nor apathetic, I supposed I felt the same way I did as we had earlier. Unconcerned with the security of our doors and windows, way out here.

I began to shut the curtains to the window in front of me, but paused at the sight of something far away. Out there, among the crowded trees in the night. Where the moonlight barely touched down. I squinted, leaning closer to the glass. Whatever it was, was big. And advancing. Closer. Closer.

Within seconds I realized several details all at once, and a slippery panic hit me hard: it was a car, speeding toward the window, at me, enlarging as it neared. Alarmingly big. My breath cut short in my throat and suddenly the car's headlights activated, blinding me. I gasped and reeled back, terrified that the vehicle was going to crash through the window, into the side of the cabin, and crush me in the process.

The back of my head struck the wall behind me, and a searing pain resounded in my skull. I slid down to the floor, legs out before me, and a brief pall of darkness washed over me.

My eyes fluttered open, warmth trickling down my nape. My head hurt like a hundred migraines piled into one boiling cauldron, the dizziness alone keeping me in place.

What the hell had *that* been?

Maybe I still needed more sleep. Since this morning, I'd only raked in sporadic siestas. Sure, I told myself, that was it.

Afterall, lucid nightmares during the *day*—

Normal, right?

I wasn't fooling myself, but somehow or another I managed to conquer the dizziness with this reassuring thought process and regather my balance. Kneading my temples briefly before finding my feet, I gingerly stood up. And reluctantly peered through the same window again. Nothing but featureless darkness, save for the dense woods barely grazed by moonlight.

My brow furrowed and, briskly, I shut the curtains. I couldn't be sure that I'd be able to conceal my vexed disposition to Leila. Not that I necessarily would want to. Afterall, I still hadn't told her the truth about my own nightmares.

Idiot.

I turned away from the window and suddenly winced. I paused and slowly reached back to touch a knot above my nape. My hand retracted, fingertips warm and wet. And red.

"Fuck," I mumbled, grimacing.

Subconsciously, the decision was made faster than even my waking self could realize.

I needed to tell Leila. Not just that I had fallen, but what I'd seen, too.

So I headed back toward the bedroom, already dreading having to wake her with troubling news. But when I turned the corner, circumventing the couch, I abruptly stopped in my tracks. I faced the kitchen and impulsively repressed the urge to vomit, or piss myself. Instead my gut just knotted up and my heartbeat felt as if it was slowing to half that of real-time.

Standing in the kitchen was someone I didn't recognize immediately. So, a stranger in the cabin was startling enough. But I didn't exclaim. I stared in awe, the man's identity slowly elucidating in my mind.

He was in his low twenties, skinny with baggy jeans and a white tank. He was burly for his size, with a chiseled face, and covered in tattoos. Stubble along his jaw, and slicked-back black hair.

Doubled over the kitchen counter snorting cocaine off his left forearm.

Shock seizing me, I nonetheless managed to take a few more steps forward. He didn't notice my presence just yet, and continued to make white lines on his forearm vanish up his nose. Only to never truly run out; as if he had an infinite supply.

An unending fix.

The addict's dream.

I stopped maybe twelve feet from him, and could discern a few notable features. Features that finally pulled every missing puzzle piece together. And I realized who he was. Or had been, long ago.

A scar crossing his left cheek, the side of him facing me. A chrome skull stud in his left earlobe. And the tattoo on his left forearm, beneath the unending lines of coke—a rectangular mirror with an ornate frame.

"Randy Berenger," I muttered, my voice dry and trembling.

He finished snorting the last line, and this time it disappeared for good. He turned to face me, and I tasted bile in the back of my throat. A grisly entry wound of a bullet hole had replaced his right eyeball. Two more blotched his torso, one on his right breast and the other several inches below it. While not actively bleeding, the entry wounds appeared fresh. The white fabric of his tanktop was shredded around the holes, and sticking to the bloody skin beneath.

This wasn't real.

But fuck me if it didn't look, *smell*, and for all intents and purposes *seem* real.

Worst of all and a better question, *why* was this happening? Why the sudden regurgitation of our past troubles? Our regrets?

Randy had been the drug dealer I'd killed with a .38 five and a half years ago. The other two guys in his group were murdered by my scoundrel "associates." Just a bunch of irrational, good-for-nothing hoodlums. As I had been. But that was the past.

"At least you didn't shoot me in the nose," he spoke, chuckling. It wasn't a man's voice, though. Inarguably, it was a woman's. But nothing like Leila's. It sounded older, perhaps of a woman in her sixties or even seventies.

Ice sprinkled down my spine.

The vehicular manslaughter. She had been an older woman. Oh, Jesus Christ, she had been—

A hand on my shoulder. It was freezing, even through my shirt. I exclaimed, wordlessly, on impulse, and turned around to face the new stranger. Half of my brain hoped it was Leila trying to wake me up from this terrible nightmare.

But it wasn't.

It was the woman I had struck with the car that night, my junkie cohorts breathing down my neck. The woman had no hair and was as pale as a ghost. I didn't mean Leila pale, but bone-white pale. White panel van pale. I meant white walls and ceilings in a brand new fucking house pale. Her eyes were missing and I found myself staring in speechless awe into the bottomless pits that were her grisly, hollow sockets. Her teeth were gone, too, leaving just her gums, bleeding over her shriveled lips.

She wore a hospital gown and stared at me with her head tilted. A dreadful grin covered her face.

"I'm glad now that I laced your last deal with acid, you two-timing faggot."

The voice gushing from her mouth was masculine. It belonged to Randy, the virility of his tone healthy and mocking.

She slinked forward, instead of stepping, and I recoiled, screaming like a little girl.

"Get away from me!" I proceeded to bark. "Get the *fuck* away from me! Now!"

"Aw, what's wrong, Luke?" The old woman's voice came out of Randy again. He stepped closer. A vile fluid not blood leaked from his missing eye. "You pissed off that we're picking your brain, that I'm the reason you had that *bad trip* those years ago, or that your regrets are finally coming to surface for what you really are?"

"That…" I swallowed a lump in my throat and shook my head. I poked a finger at him, weakly. Tears had welled up in my eyes. My voice broke as I spoke. "That doesn't make any sense."

"Oh, yes it does," Randy's voice, from the old woman. I flinched and looked over at her. "And you know it, too. Deep down inside…you *fucking* know it. And so does your lil' girlfriend."

Ever been pushed to the edge? Or over it, for that matter? Circumstances could vary. The sensation, and reaction, were always the same. Volatile. It didn't matter how many drinks you had downed, how much H or coke was in your system, whether you were tripping balls, high as a kite, or sober as a nun.

The edge, and being given that push, was like kindling a fire in someone, as if they were Bruce Banner with rabies.

I spoke from experience.

And this particular one surpassed all others.

I suddenly screamed at the top of my lungs, but I wasn't all bark and no bite. A split-second later I barreled into the old woman, tackling her to the floor. Because I knew she was just a figment of my imagination, and at any moment I would surface from this wretched nightmare.

For the time being, though, I snarled like a feral wolf, beating her down into the floorboards.

Behind me, a pair of strapping arms wrapped around my neck, and Randy pulled me to my feet. I elbowed him in the gut and managed to kick him in the groin without even turning around. To my dismay, though, he was unfazed. He merely grinned and prepared to attack me again.

So I screamed once more and, momentum recovered, threw my entire weight into his chest. He fell back, and I heard a *crack* on the floor. I sprung to my feet like a jack-in-the-box, looking around frantically.

Both Randy and the old woman were unmoving, helplessly on their backs.

Terror ran through me.

Their mouths were open, jaws widened inhumanly. No sounds came out, not at first anyway. The second I took a step back, that changed. The ensuing cacophony of sounds made it impossible to identify which sound came from which mouth. First, a wolf's howl. It quickly evolved into the dissonance of tires screeching on asphalt, and then a horn blaring through the stillness of night, punctuated by bone-shattering gunfire and finally silence.

My chest was heaving with great panic, although my feet felt like anvils on the floor.

Two long seconds passed before a new sound. It grew in volume while their bodies trembled. The sound of water bubbling, and aluminum popping. I watched the skin recede from their bones, which then turned to ash, disintegrating into the crevices of the floorboards, leaving the wood unscathed.

The bubbling of black tar heroin ceased.

My body suddenly tightened up and I fell to my hands and knees, vomiting. It wasn't much, so I dry-heaved a few more times before my throat relaxed. As much as it could. Sore, dry, and hoarse.

I wanted to call out to Leila but didn't have the power, or the voice.

My head hung low, between my shoulders, and I panted frantically. Despite the urgent gait of my pulse, my body was motionless. One could only begin to imagine how terrible my head felt, and they would be very short of the reality.

"Leila," I finally muttered. Filth dribbling from my lips. My arms grew tired and weak. My next breath was a shallow gasp. "Leila."

My arms gave out, wrapping around myself as my body fell, and I rolled onto my side.

"Lucas…oh, God, *Lucas*!"

I looked up through heavy, teary eyelids to see a blurred version of Leila hovering over me. Her face warped with concern and one of her hands ran across my face.

I knew in an instant that I wasn't dreaming.

I *hadn't been* dreaming.

"Leila," I breathed, miraculously finding a lick of hydration and stability in my voice. I blinked away the tears, my view of her clearing. "We need…"

"What? Speak up, baby. What is it? Oh, Christ, Lucas, you're bleeding. Did you hit your head? What's happening? I thought I heard you screaming."

"We need…to get the hell out of here."

I noticed Leila pick up her head and look around. She swallowed and took a deep breath. Then she curled her arms under mine and harnessed the strength to lift me to my feet.

My woman.

I panicked briefly, feeling as if I was trying to stand on water. Or quicksand. But finally my feet acquired purchase and balance returned to my limbs. I wavered a bit, with her hands spotting me, until I was able to stand on my own.

Even then, I blundered for the couch. Finally I sat down, falling in a heap, back against the cushions. Leila rushed to sit next to me.

"Look at me, Lucas. You need to tell me what's going on. You're scaring the shit outta me. And the nightmares…the one I had earlier, Lucas, it was *bad*. I just had a dream, though, and it was *nice*. It was about *us*, baby."

I noticed a weak smile part her lips.

And then it faded.

"But...before I woke up, hearing you scream or whatever, I saw something terrible." She frowned. "A face, distorted and rotting, one of the most appalling things I've ever seen. I don't know what it was, Lucas, but it made me feel *sick*. And I *am* sick. But I need to know what's going on...Lucas, please, talk to me."

"Don't cry, my love," I told her, although I knew it was inevitable. Although it was me who had shed more tears than her just now. I touched her face and she held my hand, but it slipped away after a moment. Then I spoke. I told her about my nightmare, about my very first hallucination. Her being in it, the realism, the cardinal in her mouth, the apple, the voices and the screaming and the horror of it all. I told her about just moments ago, the window and the car, even about Randy and the old woman.

Whose name still escaped me, digging scores in my mind's flesh, inflicting even more pain.

Halfway through my confession, Leila began to weep. She continued to listen, however, and her eyes never diverted from mine, even when mine did, from the shame and guilt and grief.

Her quiet sobbing, she couldn't abstain. And I didn't blame her. To be honest, I couldn't be certain who or what to blame.

The more my mind dwelled on it, though, I developed a pretty good idea.

Even if it hurt me to believe it.

VII

Leila and I sat there on the couch for some time. Balled up as if we were expecting some sort of meteor impact that would bring about Armageddon, and usher us into whatever afterlife might exist. How much time passed, exactly, was beyond me. But sometime around ten o'clock, we decided to rise. A mutual, implicit decision. Leila helped me to my feet again, and I stood with minimal support.

I eyed her up and saw that she had since pulled on her same black jeans as before, and a new but similar white tee. Snug and small, some of her midriff left exposed. I gently placed my hand on her soft stomach, and leaned closer to kiss her temple.

I noticed small wet spots that had dappled the chest of her shirt, from her tears.

A subtle frown formed on my face as I hugged her from the side.

She touched my arm and lifted her eyes to me.

"You said earlier that…that we have to get out of here." She sniffled. "Were you being serious?"

I pondered it.

The time that had passed, maybe fifteen minutes, was ample for me to collect my thoughts. But I tacked on a few more seconds to the deductions I had already made, subconsciously.

"No," I said after a moment's deliberation. "No, Leila, I wasn't…well, I just didn't know what I was saying. I was scared, I guess, that's all. And…"

I sighed deeply and shook my head. My right hand rested on the small of her back. I wanted to pull her so close that she would never leave my embrace.

"I think we're better than this, babe," I said. "Stronger. You and I. *Especially* you. And whatever is going on here, I'm not surrendering. You're the only thing I'd ever give in to."

I smiled and she did, too. Or perhaps hers came first. And then we shared a small kiss.

"We aren't leaving this place, our vacation home, just because we're losing our minds," I said, and chuckled. "I mean, if we're losing our minds, we might as well lose them together. Because without you, I'd lose it to a worse cause, and be as good as dead. Serving no purpose to anyone. But with you by my side, I can help balance you and you can help balance me. We'll steady each other out, the way we always have."

"Always and forever," she smiled.

"We'll endure this, Leila. Whatever the hell it is. And we'll emerge victorious."

"*Luctor et Emergo*," she said, her inflection flawless, almost lyrical.

I touched her cheek and leaned in to kiss her. But this time she asserted her lips first. She threw an arm around me and pressed our bodies together, closer than they had been. Two twist-ties curling about one another, the kind used in grocery stores. And whatever was in our bag had enough spice to kick up a fire on the surface of Neptune. A zest impossible to resist.

And impossible to extinguish.

"Make love to me," she whispered in my ear, grinding against me. Her right arm around the back of my neck, pulling my head down to her. I didn't resist kissing her cheek, her neck, and back to her lips when she wasn't speaking. But when I didn't respond right away, she added, her voice delicate yet powerful: "Please. Fuck me. Like it's the last time we'll ever—"

I pulled away from her, only so that I could put a finger to her lips. I then closed in on her again, and put my mouth to her ear.

"Nothing will ever be a *last time*," I murmured.

I then held my breath and took a step back from her, both hands descending to seize her waist. I lifted briefly only to set her back down a second later, having spun her around to face the other way. I pressed myself against her from behind, my left hand rising to her face, where she took a few fingers into her mouth. My right hand grabbed one of her breasts, squeezing through the fabric, pressing her upper back harder against my chest. All the while she grinded against me from below, an arch in her lower back, hips working.

I was ready long before that.

She wasn't trying to build me up; she was enjoying the fruition herself.

I heard a low moan from Leila, and removed my fingers from her mouth. They were sodden with saliva. I lowered them like an oil drill, just as she finished unfastening the front of her jeans. With assistance from my right hand, I pushed them down, and my other snaked between her crossed thighs. Snug but inviting. She writhed against me, head tilting back and hair draping over my left shoulder. My mouth caressed the right side of her face and neck, while her moans spilled toward the ceiling.

My right hand returned to her chest, but with more assertion this time. I yanked on the high neckline, hard enough to rip fabric, without cleaving it. That distinct sound was made, and Leila's neck braced against the pressure. She let out a soft moan on top of her heavier ones, as my force exposed her right breast. I seized it and handled her flesh with tactile gluttony.

Indeterminable minutes passed before I lifted her with an arm beneath her knees and another under her neck. She assisted by clinging onto me, her face enjoying the scent and taste of my jugular.

Before I'd taken my third step, she had kicked her jeans from her feet. I strode over them, like a discarded piece of armor. Minding her head and the doorway, I carried her into our room. In my wake, I kicked the door back and it slammed shut.

No particular reason why. It felt like a dramatic thing to do, and befitting, since the act awaiting us would not be blasé.

Besides, if something so desperately wished to ruin our vacation, it would have to break down the door and crash through the windows.

This was happening, and I'd be damned if it didn't. Leila could see it in my eyes, the conviction and ferocity, the lust and the love and the dripping ardor.

I dropped Leila on the bed and she bounced slightly.

She gave in to a sweep of giggles, sprawled on her back, arms and legs like mindless snakes anchored to her body. Not seeking an escape. Simply squirming in anticipation.

My shorts dropped to my ankles, and I stepped out of everything I needed to, in order to be one with Leila, bereft of barriers.

Seconds later, I was on top, and inside of, my woman. I didn't even begin slow. I charged into the fast lane like the driver of a stolen car, coppers hot on my trail, and three strikes to my name. Reckless but not devoid of devotion.

Leila's body reacted appropriately, if even "inappropriately," one might argue. Her temperature rose, playing tug-o-war with mine. Our pores poured and we glistened as if the roof had been removed by the cosmic giant outside, his clouds torrenting us in salivation.

Our flesh became oblivious to the slight cold inhabiting the cabin, not to mention surrounding it like a mile-thick moat.

I thrusted wildly, but with a notion of restraint, until I could bear it no more. Her moans carried me like an overture into the third act of our culminating union.

The energy mounted until reaching its peak within me, exploding but not releasing.

I crossed the proverbial bridge leading me to what might just be the most powerful orgasm of my life. Still, an adventure through thickets awaited me on the other side. My destination wouldn't be reached so easily.

And I dared not arrive before ensuring Leila had crossed, too.

Nearing, nonetheless, I abandoned any restraints still

clinging to me. They snapped like a fat rubberband struggling to contain something desperate to break free. And nothing, in that moment, would fucking suppress me. Nor Leila, bucking and gasping beneath me, licking the air and glimpsing the abysses behind her eyes.

It wasn't long after that she came. Shuddering in more ways than one, at depths both corporeal and immaterial, the muscles in her neck tensing visibly for the longest breath.

I felt it, too, below and within.

God, fucking, *damn* I was alive.

I all but commanded her to savor it, between panting growls, as I cherished the sight and sensation from where I pinned her to the bed. When in reality, she had given us both wings we so longed for.

Even as she began to recover, there remained a nimbus of intemperance to her. The glow of pleasure and dedication. Loyalty beyond the flesh.

She reached around me, seizing my buttocks and pulling with all her might. Tacitly demanding I not only stay inside, but make myself at home, in the farthest reaches of her fathoms.

How could I refuse such hospitality?

There wasn't a single universe in a multitude of realities where I would.

A half-smile birthed on her face, and with utmost veracity, I mirrored it.

Seconds later, there were no half-measures. Full, ear-to-ear grins awaited us on the other side of my buckshot climax. My toes curled so hard I wouldn't be shocked if they broke in the process. I wouldn't have noticed. I jettisoned into her, and she savored it with a wet four-letter word that wasn't "love" or "lust" but a hybridization of both.

There was something delicious about how her lips and teeth gnashed together the C and the K.

Finally, smiles painting our faces, we relaxed into each other's arms.

"You sure do know how to take me high," she whispered, turning to face me. She spread her fingers and ran a hand over my head. "No one else could ever take me higher."

I smiled but felt my insides tighten.

"Give me a smooch," I lightheartedly said, after a pause. A shortness of breath and an uncertainty of how to respond to such a humbling remark. Not the first time I had been on the receiving end of a compliment like that, from her, but more than ever before it struck a stronger chord inside me. I could taste her words, and feel them slither their way into the bowels of my heart.

Leila, meanwhile, simply giggled in response to *my* remark, which produced a lopsided smirk on my own face.

"What if I don't want to?" She raised an eyebrow and pursed her lips. My beautiful tease.

"And why would you wanna do that?" I asked, tilting my head. "You'd be missing out."

"Oh, yeah? On what?"

"These lips, my love," I said, parting a hair from her clammy forehead. "They are a prince's."

She tittered, only to divert her eyes briefly. When she

looked back up at me, that very same stare became supple in nature, and I wanted nothing more than to consume every morsel of it.

"No," she whispered, her face looming closer. "They are a king's, and I am your queen."

My smile began to fade. I cupped her face and neared my lips to hers, only to pause at the last second. I could hear the anticipation in her breath squeak off of her tongue.

"No, you are a goddess."

Her brow furrowed. She damn near frowned. And then she kissed me, a tidal wave of passion transmuting from her mouth to mine. But, goddammit, it originated from someplace so much deeper and intangible.

"Then…what does…that make you?" She asked, in between moist breaths.

Our chests began to collide again, as intermittently as our mouths.

"Your servant," I said, and prepared to dive back into her.

A hefty silence settled over us, conquering the music between our bodies. It heralded a worse sound, a chilling whistle of the coldest imaginable wind. The breath of something horrendous and unforgiving.

The shut window by the bed exploded inward, showering us with tiny splinters of wood and glass. I impulsively threw my arms around Leila, as she let out a kneejerk shriek. The aforementioned gust of wind had suddenly reached its icy fingers into the cabin, prickling our skin and threatening to defeat the warmth in our veins.

All the while I mumbled false reassurances into

Leila's ear.

A corner lamp crashed to the floor. The drawers to both dressers shot open, all of our clothes fountaining into the air. The vanity rattled where it stood, its mirror all but shattering in its oval frame. The wooden legs to my dresser stomped the floor in a fit, as if sentient and protesting this madness.

Or submitting to its sway.

At long last, the wind ceased its tumult and I could feel Leila tentatively relax in my arms.

I, however, had a terrible hunch that the chaos wasn't over just yet.

That it had barely even begun.

And then the door to the bedroom blew inward, right off its hinges. Both brass fixtures screamed as they slid across the floorboards. The door itself cartwheeled through the air, past the foot of the bed and in front of Leila's vanity. It crashed into the wall by the fallen lamp, but that didn't terminate its momentum. Unnaturally, it redirected its path into my dresser. The furniture tumbled sideways, raucously landing under the destroyed window.

Leila had screamed again, clinging onto me, and I had not kept quiet myself.

I also wasn't blind to the turmoil in the room, unlike Leila, who buried her face and likely begged for it to end.

Drawers, clothes, shards of wood, and glass splinters littered the bedroom floor.

My attention averted to the doorway.

Through which came new sounds. From the rest of the cabin. Their audible reach was pervasive. Loud, shrill, and undeniably violent. Glass shattering, wood cracking, light bulbs popping, even the ripping and tearing of fabric.

Actions that would take an army to commit in such little time. Certainly no earthly gust of wind, lest the whole cabin be torn from its foundation.

"What's happening, Lucas!?" Leila screamed under her breath, barely discernible.

"Something…Something's in here with us," I said, unable to mask the scary truth anymore.

"Someone," she started to say.

I shook my head vigorously.

"No. Some*thing*."

Leila struggled to grasp even a mote of what I implied.

"What?" Her eyes locked onto me. "Why?"

I swallowed a lump in my throat. I couldn't bear the strength to expose the truth to her, or at least what I had come to believe was this unnerving truth.

"I don't know," I ultimately said, which wasn't technically a lie. I stopped glancing at the doorway and bared my gaze to Leila's. Her eyes were glassy and I suddenly felt my own face contort with vehemence. A rancor not directed at her, of course, but whatever this wretched force was. "But I'm not gonna let it get to you."

I crawled off of her, and out of bed.

"Lucas…" Her voice trailed off, her hands grazing me but incapable of finding purchase.

I stood, wearing only a shirt. It was drenched with sweat. Socks on my feet. I stepped over all the clothes, avoiding more by miracle than meticulousness the pieces of glass. And not once did I think to grab a pair of trousers or pants.

A beeline to the doorway, vigor pulsing through every fiber of my being.

I could hear the wind howling like a creature of its own, in the front of the cabin. Wreaking havoc, still, to the kitchen and den.

"Don't be afraid, baby," I said, without looking over my shoulder. I didn't have to look to know that she was still on the bed. Fear held her there, not necessarily captive, but still rational.

That very virtue had abandoned me.

I exited the bedroom, heart pounding against the cage that was my chest. This wasn't bravery, mind you. This was a new shade of lunacy.

Entering that open space between the den and kitchen had me scared out of my mind, but with an iota of relief came the stillness. All of the havoc had been wrought, and upon my arrival, it simply ended. The culprits, of course, were unseen. Only the aftermath was to be taken in.

To my right, the kitchen was in ruins. Cabinet doors sundered, pots and pans and silverware strewn about. A large, impossible fissure streaked the granite countertop. The refrigerator door was off its hinges and nowhere to be seen…

No, wait, it was on the couch.

I noticed this after glancing over the kitchen, which stole my attention right away, given its vicinity. Among other things.

Such as the baker's dozen of apple cores scattered around the toppled trash bin.

We had only brought four.

The unease metastasizing in my body was only just beginning.

To my left was the den—once a remarkably cozy part of the cabin, and a place of warmth, of comfort, and of solace. Especially, if not strictly, when shared with Leila.

Now, it had been desecrated by this unnatural, unspoken violence.

The couch, besides having the refrigerator door lodged into it, was shredded. Its innards littered the den, some of it still floating in the air. The TV was face-down on the floor, shattered from screen to VCR. The few windows in the space had also been shattered, curtains shorn by glass. Every lamp in the den had fallen, their bulbs now in pieces.

It was murky and unpleasantly cold.

"Are you so cowardly as to hide yourself from me?" I suddenly asked, my voice low. I knew I didn't need to scream to be heard by my elusive enemy.

I posed the question again, still not screaming it, but this time with added vivacity.

No answer.

Just a searing wind dancing outside, through the windows. Cold as it was in here, the malicious wind no longer rampaged.

My arms dangled by my sides. Hands turned into clenched, white fists. Brow furrowed and lips creased to reveal clamped teeth. I caught my breath, somehow, slowing my heartbeat. Gaining control—just so I could lose it again.

"Goddamn you!" I bellowed, distending three syllables to the limit of my lungs.

All of a sudden I was answered, and part of me wished I hadn't been.

The floorboards beneath me rippled, like waves eddying around a giant splash. I was knocked off my feet, hitting the floor face-first; fortunately my arms managed to mitigate the impact. Nonetheless, searing pains jolted through my hands and up my arms. I grimaced and spittle sprayed from my mouth.

Struggling to rise back to my feet, I noticed a shadow—darker than the moonlit night filling the den— loom over me. My eyes widened at the sight of the couch being lifted on its right end, tilting toward me. Before I could evade, the refrigerator door crashed into the floor three feet in front of me.

I bounded back, heels scrambling, hoping I'd avoid the falling couch. Thanks to my socks and sudden loss of balance, I wound up sliding across the floor in a panic. Ultimately the couch landed on top of the refrigerator door, with a loud crash, but far from the worst sound.

An even shriller noise announced itself, piercing my ears all of a sudden. I caught myself on the island counter in the kitchen, turning my head to witness the source of the scream. But instead, I saw nothing. And if it was in fact a scream, its source was no human, and hardly any animal I had ever heard before.

The terrible sound raked the outer walls of the cabin, while bouncing off the ones inside, like a ricocheting volley of gunfire. It continued to rattle my skull, even as I dropped to my knees, clutching my ears. My eyelids slammed shut and my jaw locked up, teeth grinding.

Make it fucking stop, I pled.

When it finally faded, there was scant relief to savor. In its place grew a low groaning sound, building like a monstrous tremor, reminding me of when a jackhammer pounded concrete. Or when a train slipped off its tracks and plummeted headlong into the earth.

Louder with each passing second, until I realized where it originated.

Beneath me.

In the next instant, I heard a guttural scream from Leila in the bedroom. Alone, it sufficed to send a cascade of chills down my spine. I spun to face the doorway, already en route. Before I completed my second stride, her scream was punctuated by a loud *thump* and the sound of my own voice bawling her name.

Alas, the harrowing dissonance beneath me struck the floor from below, splitting wood and sending me straight to the ceiling.

Everything muted and blackness swallowed me whole.

VIII

Whirring, like a helicopter's rotors cutting through thin air, was what woke me up. Or at least it was the first sound my ears detected as my eyelids peeled back. Slowly, but not groggily. I had not been sleeping; I was abducted by the void for an unknown stretch of time, but I wasn't going to be kept from my love.

My body was incomparably sore, head to toe. As my eyes adjusted to the bright lighting—the what?—I tried to stretch my body out. But I couldn't. There wasn't enough space to.

A few seconds later, I realized why.

I was sitting in the stall shower, glass door shut.

"What the…?" My voice mumbled on.

I looked down and sitting in my lap was the bedside alarm clock. It wasn't plugged in, but that didn't seem to stop the digital readout from displaying a time. According to the ruby numbers, which pulsed, it was 3:05 in the morning.

Temples throbbing and a pain tickling my spine, I investigated the clock briefly, infuriated that it was working without power. Finding no explanation, I dropped the severed cord from my hand and pushed my back into the glass door behind me. I then chucked the clock at the tile wall in front of me, turning my face as it shattered.

With a rush of adrenaline, I got to my feet and only stumbled for a couple of steps, which I took out of the shower. I was completely naked, head to toe, not even my socks remained. Details which would startle and trouble most people were ones I ignored on my way to the front of the cabin.

Our bedroom had certainly seen better days.

The bed itself had been tossed against the wall, at an angle, the frame's underside exposed. Conversely, the room was devoid of debris, entirely. Not a single shard of glass or splinter of wood could be seen. The sheets, clothes, door, and furniture were still all in the same disarray. But harmful debris had vanished, and the broken window was now missing. Not just the glass but the entire window, frame and all, *gone*.

Disquieting, but I accepted it all in stride as I walked across the unscathed floor, toward the front of the cabin.

The den was so still and silent that it disturbed me more than the chaos earlier. Just like the bedroom, every single window was missing, along with every iota of debris. As if all of it had been vacuumed out through the windows, through the chimney, and left the floor essentially spotless.

A clean slate.

Through the square holes in the wall, where the windows had been, seeped moonlight. It seemed so…stark, so unabashed. Neither blinding nor dim, it illuminated the inside of the cabin with its reassuring glow.

Leila was nowhere to be seen, though.

So…not very reassuring.

The only fleck of relief was that sunup was in about

two hours. Assuming the mysterious clock was correct.

Even then, the comfort was shallow.

Afterall, so much of our dread the previous day had been during daylight.

Still, there was something alluring about witnessing the sun wake from its eleven-hour slumber. Leila and I had never been morning people. Sunsets, we had experienced in every fashion. But sunrise…

Leila.

The name, the person, the character, my love, my joy, my world, it all hit me like a locomotive. My skin crawled, my spine tingled. I turned on my heels and scrambled back into the bedroom.

Where I had left Leila.

She wasn't here, though. I had already—

Suddenly I scampered toward the overturned bed, resting against the wall and forming a sort of tent. I knelt beside the dark, slanted gap between mattress and wall. It was empty. Just a couple of pillows, and…

Clothes.

Leila's clothes.

I shook my head, shoving my fears and beliefs to the back of my mind. Banishing them into the chasms from which I hoped to never have to look into again.

My face distorted, my fists forming, and anger thundered through me.

I got to my feet and stormed back toward the doorway. What I could have sworn was someone's whisper made me stop midstride. I paused, hand on the splintered doorjamb, and looked over the bedroom again. My gaze painted every wall, every niche. Moonlight oozed through the one missing window, not illuminating each and every corner, but providing something more than darkness.

I was mutely grateful for that much.

Beyond this, I was emptied of gratitude.

I had been bereft of Leila, inexplicably. I had…

I had left her here. To face the evil myself, to be embattled and insane, by myself. But that wasn't who we were; we had vowed to do these things together, no matter what.

Guilt began to creep into my marrow.

"Face the truth," a man's whisper snaked into my skull. Chills gushed through my skin and I turned around with a jerk. The den was still empty as before.

A blur of motion in my periphery pulled my attention back into the bedroom. Brow furrowed, I slowly reentered.

My eyes caught a glimpse of something hazy in the bathroom. The mirror above the sink. I advanced, with conflicting haste and caution.

The mirror was still mounted on the wall, but it wasn't level. Askew, and warped by a web of cracks. It nonetheless still reflected. I beheld myself in its reflection, distorted from the cracks.

After today, I couldn't imagine that I wouldn't always see myself distorted in some way or another. And far more than I ever had before. The figurative aberration had become literal, through this traumatic debacle.

The more I stared into the mirror, the clearer it became, even as the moonlight behind me withdrew. My heartbeat slowed. Time melted like molasses. I grasped the front lip of the sink and leaned forward, bewildered and yet enrapt. The fright settled in puddles at my feet, methodically climbing up my legs and seeping into my nervous system. It took its sweet, diabolical time, too.

What I saw in the mirror was my reflection, but was it really me? He looked like me. The facial features, the buzz-cut, gauges, tattoos, complexion…

Wait, my complexion…

Very little of my skin was left exposed. I was doused in some kind of thick, oily, crimson fluid. It had a slight gleam to it, separate from the light behind me. And a warmth all its own, which must've been why I didn't feel cold in the bathroom. Not the slightest.

The fluid dripped, slowly and viscously, contorting my tattoos.

The sleeve on my left arm, inhabited by the wolf-headed dragon in the jungle, was now drowning in crimson. The ferns of the jungle and the scales of the dragon were bleeding. Above, where its tail reached up my arm, the full moon had become a bloodshot eyeball peering over my shoulder, watching me as if it had a mind of its own. And the anchor on my right forearm now sunk in a sea of blood, its coiling rope lifeless. It couldn't save itself, nor me, from the thick crimson. Also helpless was the figure of the boy and his trombone, now mired in blood. The flock of birds migrating from the mouth of his musical instrument were swamped by the crimson filth.

I was soaking red with it.

My chest tattoo was worst of all. The artistic nature of it had abandoned me. It seemed to scream, to howl, from beneath the dripping blood.

My gaze sank down, into the sink. Trying to rid my

sight and mind of this terrible mirage of a reflection. Bloodstains swirled down the drain, a perfect spiral hypnotizing me.

A pain in my stomach rose to my throat and I violently coughed. My hands clutched the curved sides of the bowl sink, veins and muscles in my arms flexing as I vomited into the porcelain.

No blood there, not even as I wiped my mouth with the back of a hand and weakly stood up again.

Reluctantly, I returned my eyes to the mirror before me. Instead of gawking back at myself, I only saw a black cloud where my face should have been. My torso, however, remained visible, and still saturated in blood.

Behind me, and through the black cloud, was something else. A blur of pale skin and dark hair.

Leila.

I didn't turn to look behind me, fearful she would vanish. So I just studied her in the mirror. Completely naked as well, far as I could tell. And the same as me, in the only other way.

Soaking red.

I reached out, as if drugged, to touch the fractured mirror. My fingertips passed over Leila's reflection, her features less distorted by the cracks. My hand descended down her reflection, until I realized I was touching my own shoulder, fingers making imprints in the gelatinous blood.

"Leila?" I muttered, tears glossing my eyes.

She didn't answer.

"Leila?" I asked again, this time my voice weeping quivering.

"Goodnight, Lucas," she said, as if speaking though a glob of jelly.

When Leila turned, I saw that a large patch of her skin was missing from her back. Her tattoo was gone and I could see her spinal column. It was as white as an icicle and suddenly I felt the weight of the arctic winter bear down on my shoulders.

"No!" I screamed out of dismay, my voice cracking, not unlike the mirror. Which I suddenly pounded with the base of my right fist. It shattered completely, and my hand bled. The pain, the warmth of it, was real. I turned away from the mirror and sink, expecting to witness Leila walk away. To my despair, I only caught a blur of motion. Not like someone walking just out of sight, but like an apparition dissolving into thin air.

I looked down at myself, and saw that I was as I had been, before the bloody reflection. Still naked, but unscathed. Visibly, anyway.

Except for my hand, where I had punched the mirror. And the spite in me remained.

I began to scream out again but was interrupted. Something sharp powerfully pierced my shoulder in several spots, like a dozen syringe needles with the momentum of a hand fueled by PCP. Except my attacker was unseen. Blood bubbled through my skin, an unprecedented pain itching its way through my tissue. I howled in misery, but my voice was drowned out by rage. I reached out to take blind swings at the invisible force, snarling and damn near foaming at the mouth.

In my craze, I lost my footing and dove into the floorboards. My face landed first, sending lightning bolts of pain through my skull.

Groaning, bleeding from a split lip and busted tooth, I climbed to my feet but was abruptly lifted off the floor. Extreme pressure squeezed my arms, and a metallic screeching flooded the room. Its sudden end punctuated the hurling of my body through the air, ended with a collision against the wall beside Leila's vanity. I hit it back-first, and fortunately my head didn't impact.

I fell to the floor, only a few feet to drop, but the wind was effectively knocked out of my lungs. My head tilted to the side where I was sprawled out, and through a warm pain in my mouth I bawled Leila's name. My world spun and spun with a grave madness that seemed like it would never end.

No answer.

I licked the blood from my teeth and craned my head up to peer through the doorway. From my angle, I could see part of the kitchen, but not an inch of the den.

Half of the couch, where it had crashed into the floor earlier, was visible.

Suddenly it lifted and hurtled through the air, out of my line of sight. I heard it crash into something and break.

"Lucas!" Leila's voice strained and I could hear the tears scream even louder.

I hoisted myself to my feet, shrugging off the pain, and pushed myself forward. Out of the bedroom and into the kitchen. The den. The couch had collided with the gaping door to the smaller bathroom. The broken television and scattered apple cores remained the only detritus.

In the far right corner of the den, opposite the narrow hall that led to the backdoor, stood Leila. In front of her was an illuminated lamp, its severed cord dangling beneath it, and floating in the air. Except it didn't just levitate, it brandished itself at Leila, like a weapon wielded by an unseen force. With every swipe, it splashed a yellowish glow onto the surrounding walls.

She wore an expression of pure ire, and wasn't cowering at all. All of her fear had either been shed like a snakeskin or metamorphosed into the anger she was currently enrobed in.

The lamp lashed out at Leila, and she evaded, while it slashed the walls cornering her.

It seemed to be toying with her.

And Leila wasn't going to stop resisting.

We only ever surrendered to each other.

With a deep breath, stolen from the leagues of my very being, and the uncharted territories of my lungs, I opened my mouth and belted out a scream that choked me near to death. The sound was grating and wordless, bestial and all too human at the same time.

As it wound to an end, I dropped to my knees, head bowed. Hoping I wouldn't pass out, but feeling I might. Hands on my thighs, chest and stomach heaving fiercely. Air returning to me, slowly and haggardly.

Through my own panting, I heard the crash of something metal. The lamp. Then a trembling voice that was none other than Leila's. I couldn't decipher words, but it didn't really matter.

Because I could *feel* its presence adorn me.

When I looked up, I half-expected to see her standing above me. But I didn't. I did, however, see everything for what it was. Leila, a wingless angel, and the enemy, a force of justice that existed solely to torment and seize.

It had come time to end the pain, and give in to capture.

My only hesitation was whether or not it intended to relent thereafter.

I couldn't see that it mattered, anyway.

"It's over," I growled, getting to my feet.

I never actually heard the words "not yet," but I felt them reverberate in my bones. And then it was upon me yet again, just like in the bedroom. I was lifted into the air and flung into the wall beside the front door. I could hear Leila screaming, from her corner. Elbows locked, hands into fists at her side, shouting thunderously, her face reddening.

"Please, babe, stay. It's…It's gonna be—"

Interrupted, I was suddenly lifted into the air again, and my insides lurched every time. Already emptied of sustenance, I had nothing left to purge.

Or did I?

Airborne, I knew I was going to be thrown into another wall, or perhaps be the ceiling and floor's ping-pong ball.

I stopped struggling. My body relaxed, or as much as it could. My limbs and head dangling. I essentially surrendered myself to this seemingly omnipotent force. But only physically. My mind was mine to keep for however long I could maintain a conscience. And that was something I prided on never being bereft of.

Jerkily, I was spun through the air. But not released. When I finally was, an explosive roar quaked the cabin. I hit the floor and slid across the wood, my skin bruising and abrading, until my back slammed into a wall. Impulsively I sat up, only to retch blood.

I was facing, with legs extended in front of me, where the couch had been.

The roar vacuumed out of the cabin through every window, and even tore open the front door. Shrilly, it whistled its departure. Like a thousand nails on a goddamn chalkboard.

Before the sound even stopped, all the while scrambling my brain, I noticed that Leila had left her corner. She scrambled across the room to reach me, knees falling to the floor and sliding across the wood. She didn't appear remotely fazed by any of the pain she must be experiencing.

Then again, compared to me, she was untouched.

Her sole concern seemed to be my condition, and that I straddled a thin line between life and death.

Only a miracle now could save me.

Her eyes spoke of this, except she wouldn't speak it. She wouldn't dare. And since she *was* my miracle, I didn't know how to put the notion into words.

"Lucas, Lucas, baby," she rambled, touching my bruised face with her cold hands. They were freezing. They were also tremendously, seamlessly soft. As was her voice, even when it broke with emotion. "Lucas, please, stay with me…"

Her sniffling tore into sobbing.

"I'm…I'm not…" I struggled to form the words with my bloodied mouth. She stopped herself just to take in my voice. And to savor the smallest smile I had ever given, but in that very moment it might as well have been the biggest grin. My voice, all the same, was frail; but not gone. "I'm not…going…anywhere."

She chuckled, a sound riddled with unprecedented anxiety.

I lifted my hand, and let my weak fingers float across her face, inadvertently wiping her tears. They crossed her mouth and she held them in place, kissing gently.

"Lucas…"

"Leila," I smiled, the pain in my mouth and lips keeping me from grinning. At least the breath had been reclaimed by my body and I didn't waste another second using it. "I don't want you to worry. I love you beyond words and I want you to know that you deserve anything and everything good in this world. Unfortunately…not everything *is* good. I know I've been great for you, sometimes I wish I could do more, but you—"

"Shut up," she said through a sob, her smile dissolving. "You've been more than I ever thought I could earn in this life. Why are you talking like this? What is happening? What is *going* to happen?"

I stared deep into her eyes and couldn't pluck the words to explain.

Above us, the terrible wind was still being extracted from the cabin. I knew it was going to leave, soon, and it wasn't going to leave alone.

"What's going to happen is," I said with a sigh, licking the blood from my lips and gums. "I'm going to continue to love you through every day and every night and I want you to continue loving the world as you have been—"

As I spoke, she started to shake her head.

"—love yourself, stay strong, because I know you're soaking red with the passion that is now carrying me through this."

"I…I don't…" She couldn't piece together the words herself.

Spill as my voice did, the struggle remained.

"I know, you say you don't understand." I smiled nonetheless. "But you do. You always have. And that's why you're so fucking strong. That's why I trust you, I love you, and I'm saying goodnight to you…but not for the last time. Because nothing…" I coughed painfully. "Nothing is ever a *last time*. So, Leila, my beautiful. Goodnight, love."

The wind left us to be.

Where did it go?

To take a breath. To have a split-second's recess. Because it returned in a matter of heartbeats later. The open doorway widened all of a sudden, its jambs yanked from the frame, as if a tornado was laying waste to the cabin. The walls far in front of me, and behind Leila, pulled apart, only to drift through the air in a time-suspended haze of splinters.

No screaming from either of us, just awe.

Looking over her shoulder, staring up at the sight, she squeezed my hand in hers. And then she stood, naked, my hand falling into my lap. She marched to the open doorway, despite the missing wall to the left of it. The white gleam from the moon and stars was what illuminated the grass surrounding the cabin. It gave Leila a sort of silvery outline, her skin and tattoos appearing to sparkle.

"What do you want?" She breathed, barely audible.

Seconds passed. The stillness clung to us, and occupied every existing particle.

She threw her arms back, fingers spreading and stiffening, screaming the words as her black hair gusted behind her.

"What do you want!?" It was a howl, a scream of screams. It doused me with chills, and sickened me to hear her so distraught. And she wasn't finished. "What do you fucking *waaaant*!?"

All of a sudden the walls returned to the way they were, intact and proper, not an inch of the cabin tarnished. From every window to the front door. As soon as it did, there was a subsonic *boom* and Leila crumpled to her knees. I struggled to my feet, every bit of me in pain. I only managed two strides before collapsing to all fours. I proceeded to crawl toward her.

She had been knocked down, but not out.

My Leila.

However, before I could reach her, the front door swung open, violently. Missing Leila by mere inches. It was startling, but not enough to make me recoil.

The calmness was unexpected.

Enticing, almost.

I mustered the strength to rise to my feet again, but this time with a renewed balance. I passed right by Leila. I knew it would be easier if I didn't look into her eyes, or even glimpse her face.

I also held my tongue.

I just strode through the doorway—

"Lucas," her voice, frail but not destroyed.

Fucked if I did; fucked if I didn't. I still continued,

exiting the cabin and plodding down the porch steps with my bare feet. Onto the gravel. I barely even noticed what would otherwise be great discomfort.

And then the lush grass.

Weeks from drying out and dying. If that. This autumn would precede a rough winter, I presumed.

Or…perhaps it would be beautiful.

I stood still, arms at my sides. The ferocious wind returned, this time seeming to pass right through me. I groaned out loud, but I didn't exactly make the sound myself. It was my body screaming, not my voice.

I had surrendered.

And then, just like that, the grueling wind withdrew. From my flesh, from my soul, and from the surrounding wilderness, leaving the canopies shuddering in its wake. Finally released from its claws, my entire body stiffened like a steel rod and ached beyond comprehension.

Then I fell, limply, into a heap on the grass.

Sprawled out on my side, limbs lifeless. Veins exhausted. However, I still breathed. I still lived. If only faintly.

IX

Behind and in a sense above me, I heard footsteps hurriedly approach. Down porch steps, across gravel, and then scuffing the grass. Not a single grunt of discomfort or pain, beyond the kind that surpassed flesh. That I could detect such a level of hurt before she even arrived said something of my condition, and my path. Not to mention, of the emotions exuding from her.

Leila arrived beside me, pale legs kneeling by my arms and her stunning body hovering over me.

Her eyes pierced mine and demanded to hear my words comfort her, to say everything would be alright. To lie. She knew it wasn't going to happen. She knew it, feared it, and wished it wasn't true. But it was.

"Hold me," I asked, and it was all I wanted.

Leila nodded, mute, weeping through her teeth. She lifted my torso into her arms right there on the grass. We both sat there, our bodies subjected to this horribly timed tragedy. However *necessary* or *justified* it could be viewed as, it would never be either of those things to Leila. To me, either, as much as I had forced myself to see it that way.

Even out here in the cold, our bodies' warmth kept things steady. My heartbeat had since slowed dramatically. My breathing had become that of a turtle's on its deathbed. Leila was trying to calm herself as well, a struggle given the recent trauma and the stark realization that I…

Wasn't going to make it.

Miracles were sitting this one out.

"Is it morning yet, babe?" I asked, my voice weaker than it had ever been until that very moment. I felt like an infant being born, unable to do much except think. At least my vocal chords still worked.

"Almost," she said softly, caressing my blood-caked face. "Almost."

Her hand passed over my brow, and for a molassic instant her fingers were like blinds to my eyes, curtains against the moonlit sky. Darkness briefly swathed my vision, my mind still a slowly beating sun, at the heart of which I saw Leila waiting for me.

Was this the proverbial "light at the end of the tunnel"? If so, it seemed apt. She had always been my light in the dark, my beacon of hope, a spark of butane amid the oppressive shadows.

Yet as time progressed here—a wounded snail leaving behind a sticky trail of blood—I noticed that light begin to dim. I knew for a fact, and would defend it in any dimension I might exist, that whatever followed this demise would not be the end of me forever.

As I had told Leila, nothing was ever, truly, the last time.

And while I wished that we could make love once more, kiss until the world turned crisp at its edges, I knew that the moment was scarce. It was just that—a moment. Fleeting in concept, but offering its patience to us.

For what reason, I couldn't be sure.

None of us could be.

We just had to go along for the ride. Hands inside at all times, my ass. Leila and I lived our lives to the fullest. Before we met, we had been barely surviving, riding the coattails of our regrets and traumas. When our paths collided, though, we learned from each other and developed a newfound appreciation for human life, compassion, and all the little things.

I only wished that had been enough.

Maybe in the next life it would be.

I held onto that, as a peculiar shade of darkness sunk into my mind.

"Please don't go," Leila's voice shook.

I extended an arm to curl around her. Our skin rubbed together, beckoning a most pleasant sensation, reminding me I was still alive, if even only by a thread. It was a quilt of tranquility, impossible to replicate. In that instant, all my worries evaporated. Wherever I bled from, Leila's presence secured tourniquets. An effortless panacea to my agony.

She held me close to her, refusing to let my torso slip out of her embrace and return to the grass.

Her soft breasts compressed against my chest. I could feel her heartbeat, and like a drug it turned me into its addict. I needed it, and life without it was not worth living. So where was I going?

I convinced myself that Leila would never be more than a breath away, ever.

"I love you so fucking much," she whimpered, before

her briny lips touched my collarbone. Our skin shared valleys of goosebumps. They were bathed in warmth, though, even out here.

Weakly, but with grave effort, I returned her embrace, my arms feeling as if one motion from broken.

"I love you more," I said, a joke of sorts between us. She chuckled, the insanity of grief jarring what would normally be a pleasant expression.

As time slinked by, the atmosphere thinned.

For me.

My breaths became raspier and more difficult to swallow, let alone exhale. Every time I gasped or wheezed, Leila squeezed me tighter. As if the application of pressure would mend my injuries.

Except that I knew, and I believed she did, too, that I wasn't dying strictly from mortal wounds.

In these sluggish moments, Leila swallowed her tongue and offered me silence. It was a beautiful, moving quietude. I bathed in it, absorbing the solace it offered. More stimulating than a thousand moans of sexual bliss. This, this was the sound of love.

My eyelids felt heavier and heavier.

I nonetheless realized, then, that night had faded. The dark sky was being pulled apart by dawn, like a surgeon preparing for an operation. The patient's skin was the sky, and his scalpel surely the sun. Its light became unbearable for my eyes, which was unexpected considering how long I could stare into Leila's.

Squinting against the languidly rising sun and its orange-red glow over the trees, gloom shrouded my world.

It was a soothing gloom, however, a blackness that featured much looking forward to.

Though, leaving behind Leila Pierce was no easy task. But I knew I had fought and I had loved and my time was here.

I trusted she could accept that, too, as much as she resented it.

"Leila," I said, forcing strength into my voice, and my eyes. "I will *always* love you."

My fingers caressed the tattoo dappling her back. The skin was so soft, it seemed ethereal.

I was barely still present.

"As will I," she said, and the tiny smile on her face was truer than truth itself. "Forever and ever."

Her hand glided across my face, then my chest, and I could hardly even feel the tempest of tears from my eyes. Rain for rolling hills that would never again swell with life, at least not in this realm. I cried them because my body and mind saw their necessity. Because they were the liquid exhaust of my emotions.

Leila slowly let my body back down to the grass, but not without hers. She lied with me there, entwining my legs with her own. Our bodies rubbed together, smoothly, as if friction was but a construct. We undulated not out of lust, but yearning. The craving to keep one another in the present, where everything was certain, even when it wasn't.

Whether or not Leila truly believed it, I chose to—that we would always be together, even if it wasn't in the form we most desired.

This was a step in a new direction.

Leila sniffled, and gently kissed my cheek, as she witnessed the light evacuate from my eyes.

"Let love show you the way," she said.

The last expression my mortal face would wear was a smile, thanks to Leila. A smile bathed in tears.

At that time, the night had submitted itself to the morning, and the sun's gentle radiance no longer struggled over the horizon. It poured, and painted us with its glow. I lost feeling in every part of my body, the sensation of life fleeing its mortal shell.

All color and light to my skin, to my face and eyes, vanished before Leila. She lamented softly, her arms clinging my limp body to hers.

A faint smile worked its way onto her face.

Leila stopped weeping, and even as I had passed away in her arms, I returned a kiss that she would never lose.

"Let love show you the way."

www.ingramcontent.com/pod-product-compliance
Lightning Source LLC
Chambersburg PA
CBHW071126100726
47908CB00008B/2501